THE HONEY TREE

Sparks fly when Merri Williams meets Walt Lime. She's struggling to keep Aunt Prue's riding stables afloat whilst Prue and Walt's Uncle Matt are in Dubai. To avoid bankruptcy, Merri buys more ponies and gives riding lessons to disabled children. But Walt is intent on stopping her. What is he concealing? And why has Prue gone to Dubai? 'When I return I'll tell you — until then you'll be on your own — promise you'll ask Walt for help . . . '

GLENIS WILSON

THE
HONEY TREE

Complete and Unabridged

LINFORD
Leicester

First published in Great Britain in 2009

First Linford Edition
published 2009

British Library CIP Data

Wilson, Glenis.
    The honey tree - - (Linford romance library)
    1. Riding schools- -Fiction.
    2. Love stories.
    3. Large type books.·
    I. Title II. Series
    823.9′14–dc22

    ISBN 978–1–84782–679–4

Published by
F. A. Thorpe (Publishing)
Anstey, Leicestershire

Set by Words & Graphics Ltd.
Anstey, Leicestershire
Printed and bound in Great Britain by
T. J. International Ltd., Padstow, Cornwall

This book is printed on acid-free paper

1

'Now is not the right time, I know,' began Prue in her letter, 'but believe me, Merri, there is never a 'right time' — for anything.'

Meredith Williams lifted her gaze from the fountain-penned words and stared abstractedly at the white bedroom wall. 'Too true,' she murmured.

The postman had delivered two letters this morning. They had lain innocently side by side on the mat inside the front door of the flat. Both contained the chance of a new and different life-style for Merri, but they pointed in opposite directions.

Arriving at the office Merri had hastily read Aunt Prue's letter whilst she sipped her first coffee of the day. Had read with disbelief Aunt Prue's request. The enormity of it made her hands tremble and her heart began thudding uncomfortably. She'd write back and refuse, she'd have to. It was impossible, surely Aunt Prue would see that. But then, Merri set down the coffee with a shaking hand and took a deep breath, how could she refuse?

The debt she owed her Aunt was an unpayable one. How could she repay years of unconditional love and care which had nurtured her through infancy and childhood?

Her parents' death, nearly twenty years ago in a coach smash, had left Merri, aged four, facing a bleak future. Until her father's sister, Prue, had swooped into the social services office. Merri could remember the moment vividly and swooped was the right word. With scarlet cloak billowing and flapping around her, Aunt Prue looked like a macaw.

Scooping her up, Prue buried her face in Merri's tawny-red mane of hair. Outside the rain was pouring down and the fur collar of the cloak was beaded with raindrops that sat sparkling like diamonds under the harsh artificial lighting. Aunt Prue's face was covered with drops of water too, but strangely it seemed to Merri, unlike the raindrops on the fur, these kept on trickling — more and more of them — all the way down her Aunt's cheeks.

She remembered Prue's words. 'I'm taking you home with me, darling.' And she recalled the wonderfully safe feeling which filled her whole body, taking away the horrid shivery frightenedness.

A tap sounded on the bedroom door, and Pippa, her flatmate's voice called out, 'I've fixed our meal, it was my turn tonight. Are you ready to eat?'

She hastily thrust the letter back in the concealing envelope. Such mundane things as cooking and eating hadn't even entered her head since reading the staggering contents of the mail. If she agreed to Prue's request Pippa would be the first to know, but until she'd made a final decision the letter would have to remain secret. At the moment, Merri was thankful that the on/off romance between herself and Richard had finally foundered a few weeks before. At least that was one less equation in the puzzle. She put Prue's letter down on the bedside table beside the second letter. The exciting news that contained was the answer to her dreams. Or it would have been had it been the only one delivered.

'Merri? Are you there?' Pippa called again.

'Just coming.' She opened the bedroom door. Pippa had left the kitchen door ajar and the smell of curry curled its way upward. 'Hmmm, something smells nice.' No way would she let on that right now the thought of eating held no interest whatsoever when Pippa had bothered to spend time cooking for her.

'One of my specials.' Pippa grinned. 'Thought we'd have a glass of plonk with it as well.'

'Sounds good to me.'

Later that evening, after a delicious meal followed by a lavender-scented bubble bath, Merri was tucked-up in bed cuddling her toes on a hot water bottle. Although it was late spring, outside a frost silver-rimed each blade of grass and ran icy fingers along tree branches.

She'd declined Pippa's offer to go clubbing with her. 'I've nothing suitable to wear,' she'd protested. The state of flux inside her head right now wouldn't have allowed her to relax and socialise easily but she didn't want to own up to Pippa just what a dilemma she was in.

'I'd offer you one of my dresses,' Pippa screwed up her face ruefully, 'but even the slinkiest would look like a bell-tent on you. How you keep that figure is a mystery. I mean, you put away most of your meal tonight, yet I'm at least three sizes bigger. It's not fair.' She pouted realistically and they both ended up laughing. 'Oh, do say you'll come, Merri.'

'No, not tonight, Pippa. Besides,

you're going with Robbie, I'd only be a gooseberry.'

'Rubbish. You'd soon find somebody to dance with.' But Meredith had been adamant.

Now, alone in her room, she picked up one of the letters from the bedside table. It was from Backentoft and Smythe, Chartered Accountants.

'Following your second interview, Miss Williams, we are pleased to offer you the position of Audit Senior within our firm.'

Merri's fingers tightened around the paper. It was a major career advancement. She'd worked very hard to pass the Chartered exams but, as witness this offer, it had certainly been worth it. There would have been no question in her mind about accepting the new appointment had it not been for Aunt Prue's letter. Sighing deeply, Merri dropped the Accountants' letter on top of her quilt and reaching over, retrieved her Aunt's letter.

'It's monstrous to ask it of you, but I

can't ask it of my friends, because good friends are exactly that: they are not family. And they should not be taken advantage of, whereas family members can be asked to do monstrous things. And, my darling Merri, you are the only family I have.'

What Prue didn't say was family members would agree, even if they didn't want to.

A wave of annoyance flooded her. It was too bad. If she decided to help Prue, it would mean losing the new job. Could she be selfish and tell Aunt Prue of the job offer? If she did, Merri knew no way would her aunt allow her to miss the chance of promotion. But even the thought of refusing to help made Merri feel guilty. If she took the job it would mean success on a worldly and material basis but could she live in peace with herself? No, she couldn't. No way.

The decision had made itself.

* * *

Awakening early on the Saturday morning after a surprisingly good night's sleep, Merri telephoned her aunt just after seven. Pippa had already left for the salon where she worked as a hairdresser. She was still oblivious both of the arrival of the fateful letters and Merri's decision, but she would have to be told this evening.

The phone seemed to ring for an age before a breathless Prue answered. 'Darling, lovely to hear your voice — whoops, I'm dripping all over, I was just getting out of the shower — you are prompt. I expect you only received my letter yesterday, didn't you?'

'I have to see you, Prue, talk things over. I know how busy you are, especially Saturdays, but would you mind if I came over and mucked-in then perhaps we could have a sketchy lunch together and chat?'

Prue gurgled with laughter. 'It would be more a case of mucking-out, but yes, of course. We definitely need to talk. How about bringing a toothbrush and staying overnight?'

It was enticing. Merri weakened. 'It does sound tempting, Prue. It's been so long since we last met, do you remember, it was in Stratford, when we went to the theatre?'

'Too long, darling. It was before I bought Rafters. At least . . . phew, must be at least three years. Good grief! How can time whip past?'

'Easily Aunt, when I'm studying for major exams and you're doing your own thing and setting up in business.'

'Well, it's far too long. Please, Merri, *do* come for the whole weekend. Pleeease.'

Merri laughed. 'OK. You don't have to plead, you've convinced me. I'm on my way.'

She tossed a few items of clothing into a small holdall: underwear, a spare pair of jeans and clean shirt, a sweater; stood leaning against the open wardrobe door, tapping her teeth with a fingernail, anything else? Oh yes. She ran down to the hall and opened the cupboard under the stairs, delved in the far reaches behind the hoover and an aged much-battered wicker chair — she'd had the beloved chair the whole of her life as far back as she could remember — and triumphantly tugged out a pair of sturdy wellies complete with thickly ridged soles. A good job they are sturdy, she thought; they need to be to withstand the rigours facing them at Rafter's.

Prue had been quite ecstatic on first seeing the property, had phoned Merri and enthused about it. But Merri, to her shame, had been so bogged down in accountancy studies she had not followed up Prue's urging to visit. Even after Prue had gone ahead, sold the old family house, bought Rafters and moved in, another exam was looming before Merri had completed the current one.

So far she had never seen the house. But today she would. And for her own sake, depending on the outcome of her over-lunch chat with Prue, she desperately hoped she'd like it.

Caught up by a desire to get there quickly, Merri was tempted to ignore breakfast and simply grab a hot drink and go. But common sense prompted otherwise. The morning's work was going to be long and hard, physically hard, and she was a pen-pushing mouse-clicker, or had been up to now. She'd need all the energy a good breakfast would provide.

Scoffing a bowl of cereal, Merri followed it by two hastily whipped eggs made into an omelette. Then, feeling prepared for the fray, she lugged the holdall and wellies out to Nelson, her green Nissan Micra — the car had been minus one headlight on first sight at the garage where she'd bought it — and stowed the gear on the back seat. Now, just a quick note needed for Pippa, telling her of the impromptu weekend visit to see Prue, placed conspicuously on the kitchen table and weighted down by the pepper grinder, their usual method of communication, and she would be away.

Merri, feeling like a child finishing school for the holidays and filled with excited expectation, locked the front door behind her and slid into the driving seat and backed Nelson down the drive.

She nosed the car carefully along Bingham's congested main street and through the market place. Towering above the cobbles in central splendour was the 1860 Buttercross, a well-known local landmark, symbolised on documents like the parish magazine and also incorporated in the mayoral chain of office.

Driving on, she passed the thirteenth century church of St Mary's and the sharp double bend and was heading east into the strengthening rays of the morning sun. Already it had gained enough power as it shone through the windscreen to warm the backs of Merri's hands where they lightly held the steering wheel. The silver of last night's frost had already melted from the edge of the grass verge, although beneath the boundary hedges it still gleamed whitely in the recesses where the sun couldn't penetrate. But stretching out in front, the sky was a clear pale blue. It was going to be a lovely day.

The traffic in Grantham was diabolical, but clearing the town Merri took the left hand turning and drove on through the quiet Lincolnshire countryside. *'Look for the signpost saying South Rauceby. It's on the left. The village is God's own and about two miles back in the sticks.'* Merri smiled as she thought of Prue's words. *'It's a tiny place, so don't blink.'*

It certainly was a tiny village but the approach road, almost a 'ride', would not have disgraced a stately home. The neatly mown grass verges stretched away on either side, far wider than the road itself, before reaching the tall boundary hedges and gave an air of dignified spaciousness that filled Merri with excited anticipation.

No mere metal sign gave the name but instead a uniquely individual creamy-coloured headstone carved with a sheep and a lamb proudly told strangers this was South Rauceby. But the grass had grown straggly around the base of the stone and part of the lettering was obscured. Merri drew up in the road a few yards farther on, dropped into neutral and secured the handbrake. It was just possible she'd misread the name.

Leaving the engine running she climbed out and ran back just to make sure. She dropped to her knees in the grass and smoothed down the long blades. Yes, she had read it correctly after all. Seen close to, the stonework carving was superb. She traced the outline of the lamb with her fingertip and admired the exquisite craftsman-ship. She was so engrossed she never heard the approaching vehicle until a screeching of brakes jerked her to attention. The battered old Range Rover skidded across onto the far side grass verge. Her startled gaze took in the irate, dark-haired man as he scrambled out and stormed across, limping badly. 'Oh no!' she groaned. Nelson's door had obviously not fastened when she'd got out and it had swung wide open and was now partly blocking the road. The man leaned over and banged it closed before coming up to her.

'Just what the devil do you think you're doing? Apart from breaking the law, of course,' he snapped. 'You *do* know your engine's still running?'

'Yes, yes, I know. I'm so sorry. I thought I'd shut the door.'

'Well, next time you park in the middle of the road, perhaps you'll make sure,' he said sarcastically. His dark eyes were like black glass, hard and cold.

'Look, I've said I'm sorry. What more can I say?' Merri realised she was still kneeling in the grass and at a considerable disadvantage. She scrambled up. 'I'll make sure I don't annoy you further.' She drew herself up to a full five feet two inches and marched over to Nelson, and engaged gear. As she drove off, she looked back in the wing mirror. The man was standing, hands on hips, shaking his head in disgust. He needn't have been so uptight. The door swinging open had been an accident. Still, he'd been right to remind her she was breaking the law. In future she'd know better than to leave the engine running.

She forgot about him as she entered the village. South Rauceby was so charmingly English an American tourist would have whipped out a camera and panned away ecstatically. There were dry stone walls edging pretty cottage gardens ablaze with colour before leading up intriguing little pathways to the old stone cottages themselves. Merri thrilled with delight. What a peaceful, perfect place to live. No wonder Prue had enthused about it.

Finding the village had proved easy, finding Rafters was anything but. The lane snaked and twisted, almost doubling back upon itself and becoming narrower with every turn of Nelson's wheels, but finally Merri spotted the signboard set high above the tall hawthorn hedge, and she thankfully turned in through the open gates.

Creeping up the drive in first gear with the window wound right down, she drank in all the details. At the bend where the drive split into two was a wooden post bearing the words 'Stable Yard' and pointing to the right. The other arm pointed to the much narrower left hand fork and proclaimed 'Rafters'. Merri stopped the car. She felt she wanted to walk round this last bend and stand and look at Rafters for the very first time without the barrier of the car coming between them. Why she felt this urge to commune with the cottage baffled her but accepting the strange need she climbed stiffly out and, almost holding her breath, walked the last couple of yards.

And there *was* Rafters.

She stopped abruptly taking in the spread of the creeper-clad stone walls, ornate twisty chimney and welcoming sturdy oak front door with its bottle glass panels. The tiny windows on either side of the door and tucked in under the thatch seemed to peep out to see her. 'Oh,' Merri exclaimed, transfixed, 'what an absolutely magical place!'

A beautiful perfume wafted along by the light breeze filled her nostrils. She drew in a deep breath. Immediately she was back in the body of a four year old playing in the big garden at the family home. Could almost feel the wooden slatted seat beneath her and feel the lift and rush of air as her father pushed the swing suspended from the branch of the tree. How she loved the honey tree, it was her very own name for it. It filled the air with a sweet almost overpowering smell of honey.

'It's a lime tree, gorgeous,' her father had said looked down at her, brown eyes twinkling with love and laughter.

'No,' said the four year old solemnly, shaking her head to emphasise the words, 'it's my honey tree.'

And now more than twenty years

later, here beside the cottage, stood a magnificent Lime tree, its perfume spilling out on the breeze and by a single breath, bridging the years between childhood and womanhood.

Merri stood, oblivious to everything, breathing in deeply with delight the evocative scent until a voice called, 'Darling, so you found me.'

Starting a little, Merri swung round, a wide smile curving her lips at the sound of her Aunt's voice. 'Prue . . . '

The two women flung arms about each other and hugged for joy.

'Oh it's been far too long since I've seen you.' Prue set Merri at arm's length. 'Let me look at you . . . Goodness, how you've matured; no longer a girl now but a beautiful woman.'

Merri felt the warm flush of embarrassment stain her cheeks. 'Steady on, Aunt Prue.'

'But it's true, darling. You were still just a girl last time we met and now you've gained an aura of confidence, poise, oh, I'm so proud of you, Merri.'

Prue gave her a warm kiss on the cheek.

'Well if I have, it's all thanks to you and how you brought me up. However, I think you'd better show me where I can park the car before you turn my head.'

'Ever practical, thank goodness. And you'll need to be, darling, coming to Rafters. There's always, but always, work to be done here.'

She led the way round to the rear of the cottage where a wide semicircle of gravel offered ample space for cars. At the bottom end was a disused pigsty, tumbling down and smothered with ivy. Parked close to it was an ancient black Rover with suspension seriously sagging. Rather than a reliable vehicle, it looked far more like a faithful old Labrador as it rested in the shade of the crumbling red brickwork.

'No garage, I'm afraid,' Prue said apologetically.

'No problem. Nelson is well used to sleeping out.'

'Nelson?'

Merri smiled. 'My horseless carriage. I've left him — ' A quick strident horn sounded from down the driveway.

'That'll be my stable girl, Janey, with the horsebox.'

'And I'm blocking the way?'

'Nip along, darling, and then park the car round the back here.'

Dipping into her shoulder-bag for the keys as she ran, Merri returned to the main driveway. As she turned the bend, there was a further blast on the horn and a girl leaned out of the cab window. She was as blond as Merri was tawny-red, her hair hanging below shoulder level as she craned out to see if the horn-blowing had had any effect.

'Coming,' Merri, gave a wave and panted up to the horsebox window 'Sorry about that. I'll just shift him round the back.'

'Him?'

'Nelson.' Merri lightly kicked the off-side front tyre affectionately and grinned. 'He — firstly — of the one headlight.'

Janey grinned back. 'Take heart. Mine's in much worse shape. Even so, it's better than Prue's.'

'That I can believe.' Merri slid behind the wheel and, leaving the horsebox to peel off to the right, trundled the car round onto the gravel. She parked next to the Rover, cut the engine and locked up.

She straightened and stretched happily, lifting her arms high above her head towards the cloudless sky. Not only had she loved Rafters on sight, but now it seemed, she had also made a new friend.

Her aunt appeared in the cottage doorway. 'Time for a gulp of coffee before we start the grand tour — and the hard work.'

'Right.' Merri let her arms drop against her sides and began to walk across. 'I'm coming . . . '

2

Merri stepped through the doorway and found herself in the back porch that in turn opened into the kitchen. She dropped the holdall and wellies in a corner and went through to the kitchen. An Aga slumbered against the side wall and opposite, beneath the window, sat a shallow, white stone sink fed, as a concession to modern convenience, by gleaming chromium mixer taps. Blue and white checked cushions covered the seats of the kitchen chairs and the colours were picked out in the frilled curtains at the casement depicting still, blue water upon which floated tiny white swans. In the centre of the pine table sat a vase filled with violet-blue scillas. The whole effect was tranquil, reassuring. Merri felt a surge of pure joy. This was the so-safe feeling she had felt when Prue had come to her rescue all those years ago. It was what she had hoped to find and experience at Rafters.

Something cold and wet came up behind her and nudged her hand. Startled, Merri drew her hand away quickly, glancing down. Two gentle brown eyes looked up into her face and she exclaimed with pleasure, bending to stroke the golden pelt. 'And this must be Bentley.'

The Labrador, hearing his name, shook himself and slowly waved a thick otter-like tail.

'He's been over at the stables waiting for Janey to come back. Greedy beggar. She always gives him a biscuit. Greed is his one and only vice.' Prue rumpled his coat the wrong way and he grinned dotingly up at her.

'We could have been burgled whilst you were busy munching,' she remonstrated, patting his shoulder very firmly. Bentley squeezed his eyes at her. His tail wagged faster. 'Knows he can get away with murder.' She dug into the capacious centre pocket of her apron and slipped Bentley a dog biscuit. Merri hid a smile. Prue might pretend hardness, but the dog was a dead give-away.

'But you can't beat dogs for loyalty. They outclass men any day.'

'Well, up until possibly a couple of years ago, I'd have agreed with you.' There was a twinkle in Prue's eyes. 'But now, I think I must disagree.'

'Prue?'

'All in good time.' She handed Merri a mug of steaming coffee and put a pot of honey on the table. 'Help yourself, darling. I know you prefer it to sugar.'

'Thanks.' Merri dipped a spoon into the pot and trickled honey into her coffee. Taking a sip, she sighed appreciatively. 'That tastes marvellous. However, don't you dare sidetrack, what's all this about a man?'

'Did I say anything about a man?'

'No. But you're going to, aren't you? Come on, Prue, tell.'

'All right, there is a man in my life.

And yes, he's very important to me.'

'Really?' Merri laced fingers around the coffee mug and settled down on the chair for a natter.

'Daft, isn't it, at my age?'

'Of course not. You're only in your forties.'

'True, though sometimes it feels like I'm well past it.' Her bantering tone dried up and for a moment her face was troubled. 'Especially at the end of each month.'

Merri stared at her. 'You're talking bill-paying time?'

But Prue waved a dismissive hand. 'Forget I said anything. I was just going to tell you about Matt.' Prue's mood was, as ever, mercurial. Merri remembered from childhood, Prue was never down or defeated for very long. She always bounced back, twice as bright as before, even in the face of horrendous happenings. There was no doubt she was a total romantic and hopelessly impractical most of the time. Whatever worrying thoughts had prompted her to

26

let slip even a tiny piece of bad news, it had now been neatly sidestepped in her mind.

Seeing the smile back on her aunt's face, Merri knew she couldn't dig into anything possibly financially unpleasant now when it was quite obvious, despite Prue's teasing on the subject, that she was really bursting to tell Merri all about her man. She drained the coffee and waited for further revelations.

But Prue's high spirits had returned. 'Matt's my cherry on life's cake,' she said tantalisingly. 'I've decided to leave him until last. So,' she caught Merri's hand, 'come on, I'm dying to show you around.'

Rafters was a rambling cottage originally built three hundred years ago but had since been added on to by a previous owner. The kitchen opened into a wide hall from which several doors led off together with a further narrow hall intriguingly turning a corner and leading towards the rear. Prue, in turn, flung wide the doors immediately either side of the solid oak front door. 'Sitting room and dining room, although I must admit, I don't use the dining room very much. Still, it's useful when I do have visitors, or at Christmas.'

Merri felt a stab of remorse at how long it had been since she'd visited her aunt. 'Do you have lots of friends?' she asked, hoping desperately for an affirming answer that would assuage the guilt.

'A few.' Prue patted Merri's arm sensing what she was thinking. 'Anyway, what do you think to the sitting room fireplace? Don't you just love it?'

Merri stepped into the cream-painted room and exclaimed in admiration. 'Oh, Prue, it's magnificent.'

'Isn't it just?' Prue said happily. 'It was the clincher when I was thinking of buying. I didn't know whether I'd be able to afford Rafters but when I saw that fireplace, I was determined to have the cottage.'

'What's it made from?' Merri walked across and ran her hands over the beautiful surface, stretching up above the inset dark oak mantelpiece with the gleaming horse brasses hanging down either side, and stroking the almost nacre-like face.

'I believe it's York slate. But, Merri, you should see it when I light the evening fires in the winter. All the flickering flames seem to bring out the lustre, it almost seems alive.'

'And your furniture is so right for this room. Dark oak and that gorgeous wine-red carpet, the copper kettles, the horse brasses . . . ' Merri shook her head. 'Oh, Prue, it's simply lovely.'

'I so hoped you'd like it, perhaps even . . . love it . . . just as I do, my darling.' There was a catch in Prue's voice.

Suddenly there were no words to say and the two women turned and enveloped each other in a long, long hug that said everything and more. As they drew apart, a mobile phone trilled out the first few bars of Colonel Bogey. The sudden incongruous music lightened the mood and they began to giggle. Prue fished into her pocket, drew out the phone and pressed the button. 'Oh hello, Janey. What? The vicar's arrived. He's early but then, he's keen. OK. I'll be right over.' She punched the button and looked up at Merri. 'This is where the hard work begins. Teddy Partridge has come for his Saturday hack. He's the vicar, by the way. Smashing chap. Do anything for anyone and absolutely horse-mad. Says he'd do his parishioners rounds on horseback if he could.'

'He sounds a real character.'

'He is, but then, we've quite a few eccentric customers, he's certainly not the only one.'

'Let me guess,' said Merri, following her aunt back down the hall to the kitchen. 'Would a gentleman called Matt be another?'

'Aha. Now there you're wrong.' Prue half-turned and grinned wickedly over her shoulder before going through to the back porch. 'He's certainly horse-mad too, but he has no need of riding my horses. He has plenty of his own.'

'Really?'

'Mmmm. Matt owns the livery stables which is three-quarters of a mile away in the next village, North Rauceby. Well, I say next village, but that's going by road. As the crow flies, it's a mere couple of fields away, over which the two of us have right of access for exercising the horses.'

As she was talking, Prue took down a puffa jacket from a peg in the porch shrugged into it and then thrust stockinged feet into wellingtons.

Taking her lead, Merri quickly pulled on boots too. 'Do you realise, Prue, for someone who said she was saving Matt until last, you've already told me quite a lot about him.'

'Get away with you.' Prue clicked fingers at Bentley who obediently came to heel as she locked the back door behind them. 'As yet you've absolutely no idea what Matt is like.' She looked coquettishly under her lashes at Merri. 'Actually, he's gorgeous.'

They were still laughing as they turned into the right-hand fork of the drive and headed for the stable yard.

The stables were built in an 'L' shape. Although judging by the narrow bricks, they were as old as Rafters itself, they were well-maintained. The bricks had been re-pointed fairly recently and the stable doors showed no signs of rot or wear. The yard was cleanly swept and through one of the open doors at the end of the stables, Merri could see rows of bridles and saddles on wall supports. It was all very tidy and workmanlike.

At the sound of their footsteps and voices, several horses' heads appeared over the open half-doors. There was a whickering and snorting of recognition. Merri counted: fourteen stables but only five horses looking out. 'Only five, Prue?'

'No, there's a couple of Shetland ponies as well, but they're too small to look over.'

Merri felt a niggle of disquiet. 'But there's room for quite a lot more.'

'Yes, I know. I was going to expand, buy some more horses last summer.' She hesitated. 'But it's a bit difficult . . .'

Cash flow problems, I bet, thought Merri and smiled sympathetically at her aunt.

'Anyway,' Prue said over-brightly, 'I've decided to stick with the number I have already.'

Merri resolutely pushed aside the disturbing question mark thrown up by her analytical mind and went into the tack room with Prue to meet the others.

'Janey you've already met' — the girl grinned and stuck out a hand, pumping Merri's — 'and I'd like you to meet Teddy, our vicar.'

The tall grey-haired man transferred a saddle to his left hand as he said, 'Prue's often mentioned you, my dear. It's a pleasure to meet you personally.' And he shook Merri's hand very firmly. Then cupping his hand round his mouth in a pseudo whisper said, 'But she didn't let on what a stunning-looking young woman you are.' Merri blushed furiously but the other two women fell about laughing.

'One of these days, you'll be defrocked, Teddy, if you're not careful,' spluttered Prue. 'Come on, let's have your horse tacked-up and you can burn off a bit of surplus energy.'

'Don't know why I come here.' Teddy raised despairing eyebrows at Merri. 'All she does is nag me.'

'Well if she didn't, I would,' put in Janey. 'Let's face it, Vicar, you're wicked.'

This time his eyebrows disappeared towards his hairline. 'Henpecked. That's what I am. And I'm not even married,' he moaned and trailed off after Prue, both of them disappearing into one of the stables.

'He's lovely, really.' Janey unhooked a bridle from a peg. 'Got a heart of pure gold.' She turned and reached up for a saddle.

'Let me help.' Merri lifted the saddle

down. It was surprisingly heavy and smelt wonderfully of leather and horse in equal quantities. She snuffed up the old familiar evocative smell. 'I used to ride a lot in my childhood and teens,' she said following Janey into the nearest stable where a bay horse with two white socks pushed a nuzzling nose against her shoulder. She patted the firm neck.

'This one's Crispin.' Janey deftly flicked the saddle cloth across his withers and drew it back smoothly. 'He's just about the softest one we have. Not like Poncho. Only riders who are pretty competent are allowed on *him*.'

'Do you go out in set rides or are clients allowed to go alone?' Merri humped the saddle into place and drew up the girths.

'Well, both really. But we usually book four or five out together, on an hourly basis.'

'And you ride out with them?'

'Oh yes, usually Prue does because the tuition is included in the price.'

'Have you a spare on one of today's rides? I'd very much like to go out. Get the feel of it again, you know.'

Janey flashed her a quick glance. 'Sure.' She didn't question Merri but her interest was apparent. Merri felt cross with herself. She hadn't meant to say anything. She needed to discuss the whole business with her aunt first. Now she had aroused Janey's curiosity. 'It's several years since I was around horses. I guess I need breaking in,' she said jokingly. The puzzlement cleared from Janey's face.

'Oh, I see. Yes, there's bound to be a spare on one of the four rides, we only do four a day, that's sufficient exercise for them.' Janey clicked to Crispin and they were just going through the door when there was a great clattering of steel on concrete and Teddy rode down the yard. He was seated astride an enormous chestnut cob with docked tail and powerful haunches. It rolled an eye at Crispin and flared bright red nostrils in a series of deprecating snorts as it pranced sideways past him.

'Poncho?' Merri raised her eyebrows.

'How did you guess?' Janey grinned and tied Crispin to a ring in the wall near the mounting block. 'Don't worry, though, old Teddy can handle him OK. He'll be out for two hours and give the horse a good cantering, maybe even gallop. Poncho comes back absolutely worn out usually.' Whilst she was talking, Janey had gathered another armful of tack ready for the next pony.

'Are all the clients regulars?'

'I'd say 98 per cent. We get the odd person coming to try us out but with people always on the move with their jobs, they rarely come for very long.'

'And do they all book rides, or do some have their own horse stabled here?'

'Oh no. We don't do livery. That's Matt Cooper's line of business.' She waved a free hand in the direction of the far field.

'Prue's friend?'

'She's told you then?'

Merri smiled and held the rein as Janey tied up another pony next to Crispin. 'Not in detail.'

'I don't know why she's so shy about it. After all, they're both free and single. Suppose it could be because he's quite a bit younger but that doesn't matter, does it?'

'Prue's not told me much at all, I've got to admit. But she's on a promise to later.'

They worked on down the line of stables and soon six horses were tacked up ready and waiting for their riders.

The first two or three trickled in down the drive just as the church clock began striking nine.

'Here we go,' murmured Janey and went to pull down the irons on a small fat Shetland with a mane which flowed magnificently almost halfway to his knees.

Prue had appeared in the yard looking spruce and businesslike and the clients gathered round her paying for rides whilst she allocated the horses.

One little girl, clad in jodhpurs much too large for her and clamped around her waist with a wide leather belt, stumped purposefully to the pony's head and stroked his soft nose. 'Miss Williams says I've got you today, Jacko,' she told the pony earnestly, wagging her head. 'And we c'n have a canter, 'cos she said so.'

'That sounds great, Rosie.' Janey held the pony's head. Gathering up the reins in her left hand, Rosie stuck her left foot into the iron, manfully hopping as she tried to get enough lift to swing her other leg over the saddle.

Merri boosted her up. 'There you go.'

'Have a lovely ride, sweetheart.' Rosie's mother called as she waved from the far end of the yard.

'I'm four now. I'm not a baby, y'know,' Rosie whispered conspiratorially in Merri's ear.

'Course you're not. But mummies worry, don't they?'

Rosie gave her an old-fashioned look, pushed out her bottom lip and said sagely, 'D'y'know, you're right.' She banged a small starfish hand down firmly on the top of her hard hat, causing her pigtails to stick out at right angles, kicked her heels against Jacko's fat sides and walked the pony down the yard. Merri, irresistibly reminded of the Thelwell cartoons, was hard pressed to keep a straight face.

The rest of the riders were now all mounted and with Prue leading — looking very smart in cream jodhpurs and pale blue sweat shirt with the logo 'Cornfields Stables' emblazoned across it — the nine o'clock ride pulled out.

Whilst they'd gone, Merri and Janey buckled down to mucking out the seven stables. By the time Merri had done two, her arms were aching from all the forking and her shirt and jeans were covered in dust. Pushing the mucking-out barrow down to the muck heap, she realised just how unfit she was. Janey, however, seemed to skim through the workload, her arms sweeping rhythmi-cally, digging out the soiled hay and replacing with deep, sweet-smelling clean bedding, tossing it high around the sides of the loose boxes. She made it seem so easy. Merri paused for breath before tipping the barrow and sweeping out the soiled bedding onto the heap.

'How long do you think it'll take before I'm half as fit as you?' she gasped as Janey ploughed the head of her full barrow into the side of the muck heap and shot the handles high into the air depositing the contents neatly without the need to scrape out.

'Not long, that is, if you're at it every day.' She pushed back a strand of golden hair behind her ear. 'Tell you what, you have a breather.'

'No way.' Merri made to pick up the big fork.

'No, come on. I'm serious. Break yourself in gently otherwise you'll be so stiff tomorrow you won't be able to move. Besides, there's a job wanting doing which I was getting round to but if you wouldn't mind, you could do it for me. It really would help.'

'OK. If you're sure.' Merri straightened up. 'Point me to it.'

'There're some water buckets and a pile of halters down in the forty acre that need bringing up here. They'll be heavy so take the single horsebox and just pile them all in the back. We'll need them up here for the horses later.' She gave Merri directions how to find the field entrance and was just handing over the keys to the Land Rover when she exclaimed, 'Wait a minute. Will your licence cover you?'

'No problem.' Merri took the keys from her. 'I used to drive a Ford Granada and tow a trailor with a sailing dinghy on it for a long extinct boyfriend.'

Janey grinned ruefully. 'There's a dearth of talent round here.'

'It seems I've definitely come to the wrong place.'

The field entrance was only a quarter of a mile down the lane and off a junction to the right and Merri soon had the cumbersome heavy rubber buckets emptied and loaded. Pulling away from the junction she had changed up into third and was gathering speed when at the periphery of her vision, she saw a small tabby cat stalk out from the opposite hedgerow and begin to walk across the lane. It hesitated and stopped, looking towards the vehicle. Merri accelerated. But at the last crucial moment, the cat suddenly tried to scoot across. It wasn't going to make it. The cat, clasping a wildly swinging, tiny, ginger kitten by the scruff of its neck, was severely hampered. Merri drew in a gasp of fear and her hands felt slippery with sweat where they gripped the wheel. She stamped hard on brake and clutch. Too hard.

The horsebox pulled sharply to one side. With horror, she felt the wheel wrench itself from her control and there was absolutely nothing she could do to stop it. The horsebox lurched sickeningly to the left, dragging the Land Rover with it. As the nearside wheel plunged into the ditch, it came to a juddering full stop. Shaken by the suddenness of the accident, Merri switched off the engine and fumbled for the release catch on her seat belt with fingers that felt like a bunch of carrots. Just as she managed to undo it, another vehicle came down the lane and pulled up quickly. A man scrambled out.

'Janey,' he called urgently as he ran over, 'Janey, are you all right?' Reaching the Land Rover he bent over and looked inside. 'What the . . . ?' His face hardened. 'Not you again.'

Merri's spirits sank even lower. Of all people, it had to be the man she'd had a spat with near the South Rauceby sign. She ran down the window. Before she could say anything, he stuck his head through, searching her face. 'Are you OK? Have you any injuries?' His eyes were inches away from her own. For a few seconds the hardness melted from them and caring concern replaced it.

Shaking her head, she managed to

say, 'I'm fine, really, a bit shaken but that's all.'

'Sure?'

'Yes, really.'

'Good.' He drew back and once again his eyes grew hostile and cold. 'So, perhaps you won't mind telling me why you've driven Prue William's horsebox straight into the ditch?'

'I didn't do it on purpose.' Merri felt her hackles rise. 'For goodness sake! It *was* an accident.'

'Accident?' He was scoffing now. 'I don't see another vehicle in sight, do you?'

'There wasn't one.' Angry and upset, she clenched her hands trying desperately to stop trembling. 'It was because of the cat.'

'Oh, a cat, was it?' He was openly scornful now. 'And just where is this . . . feline?'

Merri looked up and down the deserted lane.

The cat, of course, had gone.

3

The man limped off purposefully towards his vehicle. Disdain and disapproval were clearly evident in the set of his stiff shoulders and ramrod straight back.

'Wait, please.' Merri opened the Land Rover door and scrambled out. 'Don't go. I need some help . . . ' Her voice trailed away as the man opened the tailgate and drew out a heavy length of chain. Hefting it over one shoulder he walked back. Without a word he let the chain slide to the ground in a rattling clank and proceeded to hook up Merri's Land Rover. He straightened and looked at her. 'Please, you have to believe me. Truly, there was a cat.'

'Immaterial now, isn't it? Thank God there isn't a horse inside the box, that's all.'

'But how do you know?'

'Look, by now it would be kicking the sides down in panic, OK?'

'I suppose so,' she said, chastened.

'Hop in and switch her on. I'll back up and then attach the chain to my tow bar.'

Merri swung up into the driver's seat and waited for the other vehicle to begin towing. The man stuck his head out of the window and jerked a thumb up to her. At the same time he crawled forward very slowly as, link by link, the chain tightened.

Merri felt a small jolt and then concentrated upon steering as laboriously the horsebox started to shift. She almost held her breath as it rocked forward then with a sudden rush it lifted from the ditch and the wheel connected with the tarmac. Her relief at being mobile once more was short-lived as concern over the roadworthiness of the horsebox took its place. But even as she hauled on the handbrake the man walked past.

'Make sure the brakes are on good and tight.' He called out and disappeared from view round the back of the horsebox.

Merri hastily jumped out and went to join him. He was stretched full length on the ground, head and shoulders underneath the wheel arch. 'How bad is it?' She crossed her fingers.

He grunted and slid out. 'I've checked for damage to the axle.'

'And?'

'You've got away with it. There's nothing wrong.'

'Oh, thank goodness.' The very last thing she wanted to do was land Prue with any further unnecessary expense. 'Can I drive it back to the stables?'

'Yes, when you've proved to me you're authorised to.'

'My licence is fine.'

'I meant, does Prue know — and does she approve?'

Merri bit her lip. 'Well, no.'

His eyebrows lifted fractionally. 'Are you admitting you've stolen it?'

'No! Good grief, do I look like a car thief?'

He studied her minutely. Merri stood her ground and studied him back. He was not glossy magazine handsome - his craggy face, especially with his somewhat battered out-of-line nose, which she guessed had once been broken, had far more character — but he was ruggedly good-looking and most definitely all male. His hard scrutinising look became quizzical. 'The biter bit, eh? And what, or who, do you think *I* am?'

'I think you're a very tough man.' Merri wasn't going to admit that despite his directness, indeed rudeness, she found him and his masculinity very attractive. 'You're certainly no smoothie.'

'Thank heavens for that.'

'And to prove I'm no thief, I do know Janey. She has fairly long blond hair and wears a hair-band. She asked me to drive the Land Rover as a favour.'

'Describe this band. What colour is it? And whereabouts does she wear it, across the top of her head?'

'It's gold, the same colour as her hair and she wears it just above her forehead, at the start of the hairline.'

He placed hands on hips and stared at her. When the silence had stretched to an uncomfortable length and Merri felt a blush start to warm her cheeks, he abruptly swung on his heel, and limped away. Wrong-footed, she watched speechless as he climbed into his vehicle. Thoroughly annoyed now by his high-handedness, she marched up to the Range Rover and glared at him. 'You haven't answered my question. Do I take it you trust me to return the horsebox to Prue?' she snapped.

He let in the clutch and said carelessly, 'I think I'll take a chance on you.'

'Well!'

Before she could think of anything further to say, he'd put a foot down firmly on the accelerator and driven away.

Merri was still seething as she turned

right off the drive and into the stable yard. Janey was just coming out of the tack room. 'Where would you like me to park?'

'Anywhere at the far end.' She waved an arm. 'You've managed all right?'

Merri hesitated. Even though the horsebox was unscathed, it would be better if she told Janey. But the hesitation was a mistake. Janey obviously assumed there was no problem for she walked away calling over her shoulder, 'Could you just unload the buckets into the tack room, please.'

Merri reversed and parked. She'd leave it until later. Right now there was, as Prue had said, work to be done.

At twelve o'clock the last of the morning rides had returned and with the willing help from the eager youngsters, all quite besotted by ponies, the untacking and watering was completed. Leaving the animals contentedly pulling wisps of hay from hay nets, Merri and Prue with Bentley obediently trotting to heel, made their way across to Rafters' kitchen for a well-earned lunch break.

'I don't usually bother a great deal at lunchtime, to tell you the truth.' Prue laid several small wholemeal baps on the wooden breadboard and deftly sliced them.

'Then please, don't for me,' Merri said firmly. 'Fruit and cheese will be fine.'

Her aunt smiled. 'That's more or less what I'd planned, plus a mug of hot soup. You could manage some, yes? Tomato?'

'Sounds lovely. Can I help?'

'Please, darling. You'll find everything in the pantry.'

Within minutes the basic meal was ready. 'What say we eat outside in the sunshine? I've a gorgeous little sun-trap round the back on the lawn.'

'This place just keeps on getting better.' Merri grabbed a tray and loaded it with food. Bentley watched every move with total tail-wagging agreement.

'I don't usually slip him anything at meal times,' said Prue, 'but it has been known for a crumb or two to fall.'

She led the way across the gravel, past the old pig sty and down a brick pathway that led into a garden. Obviously landscaped at some earlier time, it was filled with interesting nooks and intriguing narrow pathways leading through to secluded lawns edged with trellis around which clambered rampant rose bushes covered with tiny tight buds waiting to shortly put on a display of blooms. But it was quite clear Prue was no conventional gardener for everywhere was a riotous jungle of green.

'It's like stepping back in time,' Merri breathed softly, spellbound by the wild beauty.

Prue glanced at her. 'Like a secret garden, perhaps?'

'Exactly.'

'Put the tray down over there.' She indicated a white-painted wrought iron table with small matching bench tucked into an arbour snuggled around by Syringa bushes and Pyracantha. It faced southeast and was flooded with warm sunshine.

The two women sat in easy comfortable silence and enjoyed their simple lunch, the peace of the somnolent garden wrapping itself about them. For several minutes they both ate hungrily after their demanding morning's work. Finally, Prue said, 'Let's start,' and dabbed away a stray trace of tomato soup from the corner of her mouth, 'there's so much to discuss. And I want us to enjoy this weekend together, apart from thrashing out the rough details'

'What about the finer details?' Merri sipped the last of her soup and put down her spoon. 'You know, those details you promised to tell me — about Matt.'

Prue chuckled. 'Don't worry, I haven't forgotten. I'm saving Matt for our late evening gossip. That way you can think about everything and go to sleep on it. Then you can tell me what a silly woman I am in the morning.'

'Has it occurred to you, I might possibly agree wholeheartedly?'

Prue flicked some crumbs from her lap in the direction of a cheeky Robin standing on his tall, out-of-proportion legs, head cocked, eyes bright with anticipation. With a swift flick of wings, he alighted on the grass amongst the crumbs pecking away energetically.

'It would be more than I could hope for.'

'I really don't see why.'

'I'd always thought love affairs were for the young. With someone of my age, it's not quite . . . what's the word I'm looking for . . . seemly?'

'You mean, a bit eyebrow raising?'

Prue screwed up her face and nodded. 'You're supposed to be over intense passion by now, aren't you?'

Merri looked at her aunt compassionately. The older woman was not enjoying telling her these intimate details. It had no doubt taken a lot of soul-searching to reach this point and even now she was unsure how it appeared to other people. And probably not totally convinced herself.

'I'll tell you tomorrow morning if I'm going to disown you. Now, what about those rough details . . . '

'Yes, yes of course,' Prue said with great relief, her face smoothing and relaxing, ' . . . the rough details.' Her hand dropped and found the top of Bentley's head, her fingers stroking the soft pelt. 'As you know, when you left home permanently, about three years ago, I decided to sell up. The house was really far too big for me. And to be candid, I couldn't afford to run it.'

'Prue!' Merri was aghast. 'You never said anything to me.'

'No. I didn't want to. Yes, I know it was your parents' home, your home, but if I'd told you I couldn't afford to live there on my own, what would you have done?'

'Come back.'

'Just so. And that's what I didn't want. You have your own life to lead. A house is a home, or should be, but it shouldn't be a millstone. It's a place of love and safety to return to, not a prison you cannot leave.'

'But we could have worked something out. Taken in a lodger, possibly.'

'Merri, darling,' Prue smiled gently, 'I wouldn't want to be a landlady. And something else, I was being selfish. I wanted to strike out on my own, before I was too old, do what I wanted, not carry on working for someone else in their stables. Don't you see, Merri,' there was an apprehensive almost pleading look on Prue's face now, 'selling the house not only freed you, it also gave me my freedom, too.'

A sharp twinge of remorse made Merri wince. It wasn't Prue who was being selfish, it was herself. At times like this she remembered that Prue was not her natural mother. All those years of unstinting love blurred the fact she had not been Prue's responsibility. Prue herself had taken on the role of nurturer.

For the first time Merri realised just what a sacrifice it must have been. Prue had put her own life on hold whilst she looked after her brother's child. Impulsively, Merri drew her aunt close and hugged her tightly. 'You did the right thing.' Even as she said the words, Merri knew her own decision to help Prue, although contrary to her own interests, was also the right one. In a small way she could also make a sacrifice and repay just a little of the unpayable debt she owed Prue.

Prue hugged her back. 'But am I doing the right thing now? I mean, I've given you space for the last three years and now I'm asking you to give that up for me.'

'And take over the running of the stables? That's what your letter said.'

'Basically, yes.'

'Why?'

A guarded look came over Prue's face. 'I can't tell you, Merri, not at the present time.' Her hand dropped once more to seek comfort in fondling

Bentley's soft ears. 'When I come back — definitely, when I come back — I'll tell you everything, but right now, I don't feel I can.'

'At least tell me where you're going, you didn't say in your letter.'

'Didn't I?' Prue's eyes widened. 'I must be going ga-ga. But it *was* written very hastily. Anyway,' she dropped her bombshell, 'I'm going out to Dubai.'

Merri was staggered. 'If you'd said the moon, I couldn't be more surprised,' she managed to say.

'There's a very good reason, believe me, darling. It isn't something I'm doing on a whim.'

'I wouldn't think it was. But, Dubai! It's so far away. How long will you be gone?'

'Ha, now that I'm not so sure about.' Prue frowned. 'Depending on what happens out there, it could be anything from a minimum of three or four months to ... ' she shrugged and waved a vague hand, 'possibly six.'

'Prue,' Merri said gently, 'what

happens if I meet major problems with the stables? Do I call you back? Can I call you back?'

Prue shook her head. The usual lively spark of vitality had disappeared and suddenly she looked much older. 'No.'

'But surely —'

'I'm truly sorry, Merri, it would be out of the question. That's just one of the reasons, as I said in my letter, why I cannot ask just anybody to take over for me. It's a massive commitment, and one that can't be shed. Once I board the plane for Dubai, you'll be on your own.'

Merri felt a shiver of apprehension. 'I might fail you, Prue.'

'You won't, I know you won't.'

'You're incredibly optimistic,' Merri said shakily. 'Admittedly, I know my way around horses, well, after being brought up with them through your job, I'm confident I can look after them, but I've never run a business in my life.'

'You're qualified in accountancy, you

can deal with the books, etc.'

'Ye . . . es. But there's all the buying in of stock, staff wages, decisions to be made . . . '

'Look, darling, whatever needs to be done, I give you full responsibility — and my permission — to go ahead and do it. I trust you.'

Her words should have allayed Merri's fears but instead they made her feel totally inadequate and unworthy of such absolute trust.

'Anyway,' her aunt rose to her feet, 'we need to get back to work. Shall we forget about it until this evening? Then, after supper, if you feel up to it, you can have a look at the books.'

Merri nodded. Right now, however, she didn't think she'd be up to facing food, she felt quite sick with anxiety.

Teddy was in the doorway of the tack room sitting astride a straw bale enjoying the warm sunshine and industriously cleaning tack. He was humming, matching his polishing strokes to the tune of Onward Christian Soldiers. It was more enthusiastic than tuneful because he was also nonchalantly chewing on a corn stalk. He removed the straw from between his lips when he saw them approaching. 'Three gorgeous-looking women — truly, heaven *is* on earth.'

'And I thought I was bad at adding up,' said Prue. 'You need an abacus, Teddy.'

'Not so, my dear lady.' With the piece of straw, he pointed down the yard. On cue, Janey appeared, hefting a water bucket.

Merri grinned. 'Case proved.'

'If you want to play hookey, you can, you know. Merri's here for the weekend to help me out.'

Teddy smote his chest. 'Redundant — at my tender age.'

'Nonsense, just offering you a get out, if you want one.'

'Which I don't. Horses are my second love in life, as you well know, Prudence. I don't have to tell you what my first is.'

She held up both palms and backed

away. 'OK, OK.' Edging past with exaggerated caution, she beckoned to Merri and pointed out a saddle suspended on one of the pegs. 'Could you tack up Blue Lady, her stable's down the far end, the names are all above the doors. I'll do Merrymaid. They're the only two going out this afternoon.'

Merri took the saddle down and supported it along her left arm. It smelt wonderfully of horse and the saddle flaps gleamed in the sunshine that slanted through the open door. 'Is Janey not about?'

'No, she'll have just gone; she doesn't usually work Saturday afternoons, nor on Sundays.'

'What about during the week?' Merri took down a bridle and flipped it across the saddle.

'Part-time here, and again, part-time over at Matt's.'

'We're lucky getting her on Saturday mornings then.'

'Well, yes. Except that most of Matt's clients always take their own horses out at the weekend. It's livery, you see, not riding school.'

'Hmmm, Janey was saying something along those lines to me earlier.'

'Best get tacked-up.' Prue glanced quickly at her watch. 'They're due out in ten minutes.' She followed Merri out and across the yard. 'Afraid you'll find with rides being timed, it's all clock watching. Can't afford to be late, even if the clients are, which they're not, well, not often, thank goodness. You nearly always have to pull the ride out together, you see.'

'And you want me accompanying the rides to instruct the clients when you go away?'

'That's it.' Prue looked a little anxious. 'Sure you want to go ahead?'

'Now you're offering me a get out, if I want one.' Merri patted Prue's arm. 'Like Teddy said, I don't.' She forced confidence into her voice and was relieved to see Prue relax.

They parted, each to a different stable, a different pony.

Blue Lady, a dappled grey, swung her quarters round as Merri pushed open the lower door and went in. She turned her head and blew through her wide quivering nostrils. Merri could feel the warm breath fan her cheek. Taking a deep breath, she blew down her own nose in reciprocation. Blue Lady lowered her head, whickered softly and nuzzled her arm. The so familiar, almost intoxicating smell of warm horse flowed over Merri and feeling she had indeed come home, she stroked the velvet soft nose, letting her hand stray down to smooth over the sharply contrasting stiff bristles on either side. 'You're a beauty, aren't you?' The mare whickered again. Merri slid the bit between the pony's lips and over tongue and teeth before raising the bridle over her ears and buckling the throat lash. Whilst the pony mouthed and jingled the cold bit, Merri quickly drew on the saddle cloth and cinched up the girths on the saddle. The mare blew herself out as she felt the restriction and Merri laughed softly. 'You wait,' she warned, 'I'll tighten it when you're outside, you old fraud.'

Prue popped her head over the half-door. 'I'm just going to tack-up Poncho.'

Merri raised both eyebrows. 'Dicing with death?'

'No, not really. Teddy's burned off most of his fireworks this morning. He can well stand a further hour's exercise. I though you might like to saddle Crispin and join us on the ride. What do you say?'

'Yes, please.' Merri said it without hesitation

'Thought you would.' Prue laughed. 'But after all the work this morning you'll definitely need a deep hot bath with some spa salts tonight.'

'I'll second that.' Merri undid the head collar and led Blue Lady out across the yard and tied her up. The mare tossed her head up and down, snorting with anticipation. Bending at her side, Merri swiftly tightened up the girth safely. 'Can't have the saddle slipping when your rider's on board, can we?' Blue Lady scraped a hoof impatiently on the concrete. She patted her and went to tack-up Crispin.

He was resting the offside rear hoof and dozing in his stable. 'Come on, old chap.' He yawned widely, curling lips back from formidable teeth. 'Sorry, but I'm riding you out this afternoon.' He closed his jaws and gave a vigorous shake. Deftly, Merri saddled up. 'You ought to be highly honoured, you know. This will be the first time I've been on horseback for at least three years.'

But as soon as the ride pulled out, trotting in single file down the lane, Prue leading the two young clients with Crispin bringing up the rear, riding came back as naturally as breathing to Merri. She applied pressure with her knees, rising to the trot, and felt the creak of leather saddle flaps above rhythmically moving withers and it was all so familiar.

The three year gap might never have been, so in tune was she with the horse. A feeling of freedom and exhilaration rose up. Why on earth had she left it so long? All the negative doubts faded away before the happiness and confidence that flooded her. Running the stables until Prue returned from Dubai was going to be no sacrifice at all.

Up ahead, Prue turned in at the gateway of the forty-acre and led the ride in a smooth controlled canter around the perimeter. With the green turf flashing away beneath Crispin's hooves and the breeze whipping both the horse's mane and her cheeks, Merri's spirits soared, she was going to really enjoy the next few months.

As they lined up beside the gate ready for a steady, cooling down hack back to the stables, a battered old Range Rover drew up alongside and the driver raised a hand in greeting to Prue. Merri's heart began to beat faster with apprehension. She recognised the vehicle — and its driver. It was the man who had towed the horsebox out of the ditch.

A horrible thought entered her head. Could this man actually be Matt? Surely not. She felt a strange sinking sensation in her stomach and found her hands gripping Crispin's reins far too tightly, betraying and transmitting her tension to the horse which began playing up. Janey had let slip that Matt was a good deal younger than Prue. But surely it couldn't be him. Illogically, she found herself holding her breath and desperately hoping this wasn't Matt. But with the man's opening words, she released her breath in a huge sigh of relief.

Totally ignoring her, he spoke to Prue. 'Delivered verbatim, a message from Matt — 'You're to come for lunch at one o'clock tomorrow, and a refusal is not an option.' '

'My, he is getting masterful,' Prue said. 'Do I take it that includes my niece, Meredith, as well?'

The man turned his gaze on Merri.

'So,' he drawled, 'that explains who you are.'

Their eyes met — and held. Merri's heart began beating faster again, but this time it wasn't from apprehension.

Still looking intently at her, he said, 'I would say Meredith's refusal is not an option either.'

4

'I'm so glad I twisted your arm.' Merri contentedly sipped her after-dinner coffee and watched the flames from the log fire reach upwards with long flickering golden fingers. Their images reflected in the convex sides of the copper kettles on either side of the hearth which in turn reflected bright dancing forms upon the nacre-like surface of the fireplace. A log slipped, crackled, and settled with a soft sough.

'What a treat.' She stretched out stockinged toes to the warmth and wriggled deep into the cosy armchair.

'I don't know about a treat,' said Prue. 'It may be the end of May but, my word, it does drop down cold in the evenings. Shouldn't be surprised if there's another frost tonight.'

But Merri was dreamily watching the flames. 'It would be impossible to capture this in a painting, or even in a photograph,' she murmured. 'But you're quite right, Prue, the fireplace really looks alive. One thing, though . . . '

'And what's that?'

'Well, Bentley's snoring on the hearthrug but you ought to have a cat purring on your lap.'

'You could be right,' Prue reached across to the log box and dropped another log on the fire. 'However, since I'll be leaving for Dubai in a week's time, the cat will have to wait until I get back.' She picked up the coffee jug and inclined her head in query.

'Oh yes, please. I don't think there's any chance of it keeping me awake tonight. I'm deliciously tired, happy, satisfyingly tired, you know what I mean?'

Prue nodded, 'The best way of getting a good night's sleep, lots of hard physical work — without stress.' She poured two coffees and settled back in her chair.

'Now,' said Merri impishly, looking

sideways at her, 'I'm waiting to hear all about the cherry on your cake.'

'My . . . ?' Prue broke off, laughing. 'You mean, Matt.'

'Indeed I do. Come on, Prue, give.'

'Almost exactly a year ago, I was introduced to Matt by his father, Walter Chessington. Of course, I knew Walter a couple of years before that because he was the founder of Chessington's Livery.'

'The stables in North Rauceby?'

'That's right. Walter and Hilda, his wife, were friends, good friends. They asked Mr Bentland, the farmer, who owns the forty-acre, if I could use it for exercising the horses. Anyway, Mr Bentland was big-hearted enough to agree to me using it as well as Walter.'

'I suppose being almost on the doorstep, it's a great help.'

'It's made all the difference, Merri. It means I can squeeze in one additional hour's ride. And believe me, one extra hour's income from the stables really counts.'

Merri deliberately avoided looking at her aunt and instead drained her coffee. She was sure, even before she scrutinised the books that the stable was barely paying its way. Pushing aside the worry until later, she gently nudged Prue back to the intriguing subject of Matt.

'Walter had his seventy-fifth birthday at the end of May last year. There was a bit of a party, a few friends from the village, relatives, you know. Matt couldn't make it though. Apparently he had an important race right at the end of the season which he didn't want to miss. He was a jump jockey, by the way. Well, at the party Walter surprised everybody when he told us he and Hilda were giving up the stables and going to live near their daughter in Yorkshire.

'A couple of weeks later Matt arrived. It was the day of the village flower show and Walter introduced him to me. The rest is history.'

'Not to me it isn't. OK, that's the

background, but tell me about Matt himself.'

Prue coloured a little. 'What can I tell you? He's thirty-eight, average height, has brown hair, grey eyes, just normal, I suppose.'

'No way. Not if he's the man for you, Aunt Prue. He must be pretty special. I mean, I'm not being nasty in the slightest, but you've never bothered with men before. All those years I lived at home with you there were never any boyfriends that I can recall.'

Prue smiled a little sadly. 'No, my darling. You were my priority.'

Merri caught her breath. 'Wait a minute, do you mean you could have had boyfriends, if it hadn't been for me?'

Now she'd asked, she was suddenly afraid of the answer. Perhaps Prue's sacrifice had an even higher price than she'd thought.

'It really doesn't matter, does it? Not after all this time. Whatever I may or may not have missed out on in my younger days, I've been recompensed a hundredfold now I have Matt.'

'I was right, then, wasn't I, he is very special?'

'As special as it can get.'

Prue couldn't meet Merri's eyes and her cheeks flamed crimson. An intense, charged silence followed her words. Merri felt a flash of jealousy. It startled her. Jealousy was not a feeling she normally ever experienced — or wanted to. She was acutely aware of an indefinable sense of double loss. A loss of something she already had and also of missing out on something of stupendous worth which she had never had. But almost immediately, she felt so very ashamed of herself.

Quickly smothering the jealousy, she reached across and gently put a hand on her aunt's arm. 'Dearest Prue, if you're trying to say you love Matt, there's no need to be embarrassed, just say it. I'm delighted for you.'

'Truly?'

Merri nodded. 'I've always looked

upon you as a mum, as well as an aunt, a sister and most of all, a best friend, but those were ties of love. It would be incredibly selfish of me to begrudge you having someone else to love.'

Prue lifted her gaze to Merri's face. 'My darling.' Her eyes filled with tears. 'I love Matt so much, but it doesn't mean I love you any less.'

'I know, I know,' Merri patted her arm. 'It's just rather a shock.'

'And you don't think I'm being a silly woman? You see, Matt's eight years younger than me. It's a lot. I suppose he's what people will call a toy-boy.'

'I doubt that. You say he was a jump jockey, yes?' Prue nodded. 'Then he's tough, a real man. There's no 'boy' about it. And I certainly don't think you're being silly. If he feels the same way about you, that's all that need be said. No way would I try and come between you. You're a lucky lady to have found such love and I'm thrilled it's happened. No one deserves happiness more than you do.'

'I'm so relieved you've taken it like this.' Prue dabbed away the tears. 'And I can't wait for you to meet him tomorrow.'

'Me too.' Even as she said it, she had a mental picture of the man who drove the battered Range Rover. He must surely be a friend of Matt's to be passing on such a personal invitation. Merri felt a tingle of attraction as she pictured his face, the look in his eyes, then chided herself for being silly. She must have imagined a flash of interest. For goodness sake, he was certainly no sweet-talking ladies' man. On the contrary, up until that moment, he'd shown her nothing but a hostile brusqueness. And anyway, even if he was a friend of Matt's, it didn't mean she would be meeting the man again.

Her aunt's voice broke in, effectively and immediately, banishing all other thoughts. 'If you've finished coffee, Merri, would you care to have a look at the stable books now?'

Going over to the table where they

were laid out ready, Merri sat down, her heart sinking as well. She had been dreading finding out the true state of her aunt's business. Although the figures before her confirmed her suspicions, they were not quite as bad as she'd feared.

'How are you getting on?' Prue came and stood behind her, looking over Merri's shoulder at the ledger. 'Shall we live to fight another day?'

'You want the truth?'

'Of course.'

'If the stables go on as they are doing, you'll be out of business in another year.'

'I've got that long left?' Prue attempted a joke.

'Sorry, Prue, but you'll have to think of something. You'll be facing a severe cash flow problem shortly.'

'Darling, what I *have* to do is go to Dubai. Whatever you think needs doing for the good of the stables, go ahead and do it. I'm sure you'll manage beautifully.'

Merri sighed heavily. She loved her aunt very much but she had to admit Prue was hopelessly impractical. Obviously, the stables needed a massive shake-up to restore financial viability. And equally obvious, it would be her hands doing the shaking.

★　★　★

The grandfather clock in the hall sonorously struck twelve o'clock as Prue unlocked the back door at the end of Sunday morning stables.

'Who's first for the shower?' she asked.

'I'll grab a coffee if you'd like to go up.'

'OK, shan't be long. Just sluice off the smell of the nags. Not that Matt would mind. He loves his horses.'

'I know someone else who does, too. So, what now about that saying opposites attract?'

Prue laughed as she ran upstairs. Her voice floated back, 'They got it wrong.'

Just before one, as they were preparing to leave, the front door bell rang.

'Who on earth's that?' Prue frowned.

'I'll go.' Merri went down the hall and opened the door. 'Oh!' Involuntarily her hand flew to her mouth in surprise. It was the Range Rover driver.

'Matt asked me to come round and pick you up.'

Merri swallowed hard. 'Right.'

'I'm parked at the signpost, OK?' He turned to go.

'Er . . . yes, thanks.' She closed the door, annoyed to find her pulse had quickened.

'Who was it?' Prue called.

'I don't know, but Matt sent him to drive us over.'

'The same one who passed on the invitation?' Merri nodded. 'Then don't let's keep him waiting.'

Arriving at the driveway junction, Prue took one look at the enormous curly-coated dog hogging the front passenger seat and said, 'We'll hop in the back.' She nodded towards the dog, 'You can introduce us. Oh, and I don't think my niece knows your name either.' She turned to Merri. 'This is Matt's nephew, his sister's son, Walt.'

He thrust a right hand through the open window. 'Hello, Meredith. It's about time we were formally introduced, don't you think?'

She nodded, holding her hand out. Walt gripped it so firmly, she could feel the callouses on his palm, the latent strength. She also felt a tingling current run through her at his touch and withdrew her hand smartly.

Prue had already climbed into the vehicle, and Merri hastily followed.

'So, Walt, whose is the dog? Or should I say, what is the dog? I've never seen one like that before.'

He put an arm around the big animal and gave it a quick hug. 'This is my best girl, and don't laugh, well, you're allowed just one, she's a Labradoodle.'

'A what?' Prue's face screwed up.

'A cross between a Labrador and a

Standard Poodle. Her name's Gypsy.'

'I've never heard of them. Have you, Merri?'

'No. But she's gorgeous. All those big white curls, she looks as though she's covered in snowflakes. Are they very rare?'

'Yes. I had to wait nearly two years to reach the top of the waiting list for a puppy.'

'But was it worth it?'

He twisted in his seat and smiled over his shoulder at them. 'She gives me two hundred per cent love and loyalty. Top that.'

Merri couldn't even have begun to try. All she was aware of was Walt's face and the effect his high voltage smile had upon her.

The old vehicle rattled along the lane and within five minutes they were turning in at Chessington's Livery. Matt came striding across the stable yard to greet them. He embraced Prue and kissed her in a tender, yet starving way as though they'd been apart for a year.

Merri was uncomfortably aware of a tiny flicker of jealousy that was gone almost instantly. There was no doubt that the love Prue and Matt shared was the real thing, an almost tangible current joined them. And equally, Merri was in no doubt she wanted the same depth of love. It brought into focus how mediocre had been the romance between herself and Richard which had predictably withered and died.

Prue managed to extricate herself from Matt's arms and a little breathlessly, introduced Merri.

'So, this is little Merri, a cracker, just like her aunt.' He caught her hand and shook it enthusiastically.

Merri liked him immediately. There was a happy, sincere openness about him. She felt, with great relief, she could trust him not to hurt Prue. 'And Janey told me there was a dearth of talent around here. What a pity Prue found you first.'

'It is, isn't it? A crying shame.'

'I could always stand aside.' Prue called his bluff.

'And have him accused of cradle-snatching?' Walt entered into the spirit of things.

'Do you know, I should have thought he'd already got that reputation with Janey.'

'I think it's time we all went in for lunch.' Matt cupped his palm firmly under Prue's elbow and led her away across the yard to the house.

The light, happy atmosphere continued throughout the starter of Galia melon followed by roast lamb, minted peas and new potatoes. And long before the strawberry cheesecake — which, although obviously shop-bought, was absolutely delicious — Merri had lost all her apprehension about Walt and was relaxed and thoroughly enjoying the food and the company.

'I can run to cheese and biscuits if anyone has a space left to fill.' Matt leaned back looking totally replete and patted his stomach. 'But for myself, I'm packed to the gunwales.'

'That goes for me too.' Walt neatly placed knife and fork down on his plate. 'I'm really going to miss your cooking when you've hopped over to Dubai.'

'And what about the ladies, can either of you manage anything else? There's Cheddar and Stilton on offer.'

'Huh . . . huh.' Merri swallowed the last spoonful of cheesecake and shook her head. 'That was a lovely meal, any more would be sheer gluttony.'

Prue held up a palm. 'Are you trying to get me fat, Matt Chessington?'

'No way. Can't risk you being overweight. The plane will never be able to take off.'

Prue disdainfully pushed her nose in the air. 'Away with you my man and make the coffee.' Then she spoilt the effect by adding, 'It is four by the way isn't it, everyone?' Merri and Walt nodded. Matt went out chuckling.

Prue pushed back her chair and rose to follow. 'I'd better give him a hand.'

'If you're not back in half-an-hour, I'm coming in,' Walt threatened.

'You know your trouble, you're just plain jealous.'

'Not plain, Prue,' he called after her, 'absolutely emerald-eyed.'

Merri giggled. She was enjoying being part of this unexpected foursome. It was ironic that after three years away from Prue, she should rediscover the pleasure of her aunt's company when in a few days' time it would be once again only a precious memory. She became aware of Walt's gaze. He was sitting with an elbow on the table chin cupped in one hand studying her face.

'Did you know,' he said, 'when you giggle like that your cheeks dimple? It's very fetching.'

At his unexpected words Merri felt a frisson of pleasure run through her. It was not the usual twenty-first century chat-up line but instead it was charmingly old world and most romantic. To hide what she was really feeling, she said flippantly, 'That's one out of the dolly-tub.'

'So, I'm an old-fashioned guy at heart.'

'You'll be telling me you're a pipe and slippers man next.'

'Afraid not. Don't smoke myself. But enough about me. What about you? What's your normal gainful occupation?'

'Very boring. I'm training to become an accountant.'

'You can come and look at my books anytime then.'

'As a chat-up line that's got to rate zero minus.'

He leaned back in his chair and laughed out loud. 'And do you think that's what I'm doing, chatting you up?'

'I wouldn't know. It's been a long time since anybody tried to.'

'Then they all want their eyes testing where you come from.' As he said it there was a warmth in his eyes that hadn't been there before.

'Compliments, now. And I thought you had me down for yet another foolish female.'

'Well it certainly applies to your

standard of driving. I mean, come on, all the rubbish about there being a cat that caused you to run into the ditch. I know you had to think up an excuse quickly but that one's weak in anybody's book.'

'Excuse me.' Merri's eyebrows lifted. 'It happened to be the truth.'

'Oh come on, you made the story up on the spot. Admit it.'

'No way.' Thoroughly irritated now, Merri scowled at him, just as Matt and Prue entered the room with the tray of coffee.

'You two getting on all right?' Matt glanced quickly at them both. 'We thought we could hear laughter.' He put the tray down on the table and Prue began pouring out.

Grinning wickedly, Walt deliberately baited Merri. 'Do I take no way to mean you didn't make up the story or, no way you're going to admit it?'

Merri refused to rise to his provocation. Instead, she accepted a cup of coffee and the offer of a spoonful of honey. 'Thanks, Prue.'

Matt had been observing them and now subtly pulled rank. 'Are you tormenting our guest *young* Walt?'

'Certainly not, *Uncle*. As if I would.' He in turn accepted a coffee, black and sugarless.

Merri, confused and still irritated, thought his choice probably correctly summed him up.

Prue, picking up the somewhat strained atmosphere, plumped down onto the settee and adroitly steered conversation into safer waters. She patted the cushion beside her. 'Come and sit with me, Merri, have a comfortable seat whilst you enjoy your coffee. You've earned it. We've gone through a load of work this morning — and we've still got the afternoon to get through. Weekends are definitely our busiest time.'

'That's certainly where the two businesses differ.' Matt motioned Walt to the opposite wing chair by the fire and sat down himself, stretching out long legs to the warmth of the bright fire. 'When are you actually moving into Rafters, Merri?' She shot a quick glance sideways at her aunt.

'Matt knew I'd approached you about taking over the running of things until I can get back.'

'And from how Prue described you to me, I didn't think you would be the sort to let her down, not when she badly needs help.'

'And I'm not going to.' Merri took a sip of coffee. 'I'd thought next Friday, if that's soon enough.'

'Darling, that would be super. I'd really like you to settle in before Saturday so that you can join us all at the village show. There are people going I'd like you to meet.'

'Is this the one you were telling me about last night?'

'That's right. I want to introduce you to several people who can help whilst I'm away, well, if you need help, of course. But I've told Matt just how capable you are.'

There was a barely subdued snort of

laughter from Walt which earned him a frown from Matt.

'I sincerely hope you'll feel comfortable enough to call on Walt at any time if you run into difficulties when your aunt and I aren't here.'

'She seems quite good at running into things,' Walt murmured softly, his face half obscured by the wing of the chair. 'But perhaps she's one of those females who likes being rescued.'

'I sincerely hope I won't need any rescuing,' Merri said tartly and, hearing his soft laughter, immediately regretted rising to his gentle taunts.

Ever the peacekeeper, Prue said, 'I'm sure you'll manage beautifully. But now,' she rose to her feet, 'I'm going to be really nasty and leave you with all the dirty dishes, Matt. Merri and I have work to do elsewhere.'

Walt was on his feet instantly. 'I'll run you both back.'

Prue touched his arm briefly. 'Thanks.' She smiled, 'You'll have to be careful. You could lose your tough-guy reputation.'

'No chance. It's taken years to build up. Besides since I'm no ladies' man why do you think I'm offering? It's not to save you girls walking, it's simply to get me out of washing-up.'

'That I can believe,' Merri said dryly.

'Now, now,' Matt chided. 'You two will have to get on whilst Prue and I are away, so you may as well start now.'

'Can we resume hostilities when you get back, Uncle Matt?'

'Why bother?' Merri said. 'It would probably be easier if we simply avoid each other from now on.'

'Enough of the in-fighting,' Prue walked to the door, 'work awaits.'

'Thanks for a lovely meal, Matt,' Merri said. 'No doubt I'll see you next weekend, before you go off to Dubai.'

'You will indeed. Your initiation ceremony's on Saturday.' And in response to her puzzled look, he added, 'The annual village show.'

5

As Merri entered the outskirts of Bingham, the sound of church bells floated in through the partially opened car window. Pulling in safely over the crest of the hill, she let down the window fully and cut Nelson's engine. The glorious pealing of bells rising from the church down in the hollow flooded the car and filled Merri with hope and a surety that what she was about to do really was the right thing.

She had lived here for three years now, had put down roots and made it her home. It was going to be a wrench to leave. But from the moment she'd finished going through Prue's books at the stables, she'd known there was only one possibility if Rafters was to be saved. However much it cost her in emotional terms, Merri knew it was a step she had to take.

But there was an additional difficulty to deal with first. She had to return and face Pippa, her flatmate, and break what she knew would be most unwelcome news. It was going to be very hard telling Pippa that she'd have to find somewhere else to live because Merri had no option other than to sell up. But however hard, it had to be done. There was simply no other way to raise the amount of money needed to float the stables back to viability. It wasn't a case of just a few thousand pounds it was a considerable amount.

The bells pealed out over the quiet countryside in a magnificent finale and then into the silence one lone bell tolled, urging any stragglers to hurry and reach the church door before evening service began. It was almost half-past six. Merri had phoned Pippa from Rafters and told her she'd be back in Bingham by six o'clock.

Sighing gustily, knowing the bad news could wait no longer, she switched on the car engine and cruised down the hill to the house.

'I was just beginning to wonder where you'd got to,' Pippa, wrapped in a dark blue and white striped apron, popped her head round the kitchen door when she heard the front door open and Merri's footsteps in the hall. She waved a wooden spoon in the air. 'I've knocked up some Succotash, do you fancy some?'

'Do I!' Merri dragged her holdall further into the hall. Her conscience smote her sharply at what she had to say to Pippa when her friend had a lovely meal ready to greet her.

'Actually,' Pippa grimaced shame-facedly, 'it's really a peace offering.'

Merri slid out of her jacket and hung it up, 'Oh, why's that?'

'I've got something to tell you,' Pippa confessed. 'And you won't like it.'

'Life's full of coincidences. I've something important to tell you, and I'll guarantee you won't like it either.'

The two girls stared at each other and then burst out laughing.

'Tell you what,' Pippa said, 'let's have our meal and enjoy it before we rubbish the rest of the evening.'

Merri gave her an affectionate hug. 'Couldn't agree more.'

Much later, after the dinner and dishes had been despatched, the first with enthusiasm, the latter with a great deal less, both girls took dark chocolate mints and coffee through to the sitting room.

'It's just no good,' Pippa began, 'I shall have to come clean and tell you — '

'Please,' Merri hastily swallowed the after-dinner mint she'd been nibbling, 'before you do, Pippa, I've some really awful news, yours couldn't possibly be as bad I'm sure. So let's get the worst out of the way first, shall we? That way yours won't seem so bad.'

'Well, I wouldn't bank on it.'

'Brace yourself, this is going to come as a shock.' Merri bit her lip anxiously. She hated the thought of hurting Pippa, indeed would have done anything to avoid it, but knew she had absolutely no choice.

Pippa, watching her friend struggling hard to get the difficult words out, put down her coffee and went over and sat next to her. 'Just stop agonising, Merri and tell me what's troubling you so much.'

'O.K. Straight from the gun barrels, I've got to sell this house which means you'll have to move out, find somewhere else to live. There, now I've said it and, believe me, Pippa, I'm so, so sorry.'

But Pippa's reaction, far from shocked disbelief, was to throw her head back and laugh out loud. 'Oh that's priceless, really it is,' she gurgled.

'Well, if you can see something funny, share the joke because I'm darned if I can. I'm being serious you know, Pippa, it's not simply a wind-up.'

'There's no joke, not really, but it's so ironic. The news I was going to tell you was, I'm sorry, but I'm moving out.'

'Oh.' Merri was completely taken

aback. 'But why, what reason . . . ?'

'What usually comes between girl-friends? A man. Or, in my case, Robbie.' Her face coloured a little. 'Oh, Merri, he's asked me to move in with him, become his partner. Isn't it fabulous?'

Merri took one look at Pippa's face, saw the blissful happiness and said, 'I'm so pleased for you, truly I am. Does it mean there might be wedding bells at some later date?'

Pippa giggled, 'I'm hoping so. If we can still stand each other, of course, once we're living in the same house.'

'I think this calls for some fresh hot coffee. We'll drink a toast to coinci-dences. What a blessing things worked out like this. I was dying at the thought of telling you to leave.'

'Even if I hadn't already decided to move, I'd have been glad to if it helps. But tell me,' Pippa stood up, 'why have you got to sell-up?'

'Because if I don't, Rafters will go down the drain. You know, I told you over the phone, they're the stables that belong to my Aunt Prue, where I stayed over the weekend.'

'So, you're prepared to sacrifice your own home?'

'If Rafters goes, Aunt Prue goes too.'

'But, Merri, Prue isn't your responsibility, is she?'

'Not really, no,' Merri sighed, 'but neither was I her responsibility at the tender age of four with a whole lifetime of growing up still to do. But she stepped in and did it. That was commitment with a big 'C'.'

'Point taken.'

'And talking of sacrifices, I'm only now beginning to take in the scale of sacrifices Prue made whilst she was taking care of me. You don't notice, obviously, when you're a child, but now I can see Prue put her whole life on hold to bring me up. And just at the age when she could have begun to fly in her own chosen direction if she'd been unencumbered.'

'Rather like you now, wouldn't you

say?' Pippa grinned impishly.

'O.K., yes, granted,' Merri said, 'but do you know, I've enjoyed myself enormously this weekend. It's like I'm rediscovering Prue, not as my aunt, but as a personality in her own right. It's wonderful. My childhood has gone, finished completely along with my childish conception of Prue and instead my adult self has found a true friend that I've had for years but never realised. Rather weird but exciting at the same time.'

Pippa nodded. 'I can see what you're getting at. Still, what happens next?'

'I'm sorry, of course I've not told you everything, have I? Well, Prue and her gentleman friend, Matt, are going over to Dubai for several months and she's asked me to take over the running of the stables whilst she's gone.'

'I see.'

'The trouble is, Rafters needs a cash boost and completely re-organising.'

'Sounds like some project. Do you think you can handle it?'

'Not sure, to be honest, but I'm going to give it my best shot.'

'Well I wish you all the luck and then some. It sounds like you'll need it.'

'Hmmm, I'm sure I shall, too. But it's thrilling as well as scary, Pippa, a real challenge.'

'Hang on, though, what will you do when your Aunt gets back from Dubai? Where will that leave you?'

'I hadn't looked that far ahead.'

'Don't you think you should?' Pippa asked gently.

'From a common sense viewpoint, yes, I agree with you but I'm going to concentrate fully on making the business sound and let the future take care of itself. All I know is I've been given the chance to make amends for all Prue so selflessly gave me. These last two days have been an eye-opener and I'm just so grateful to be able to do this for her. If I can pull the stables round, make them really thriving, and hand them back to her when she returns, it will be ample reward.'

'I can almost see the fire and smoke coming out of your nostrils.'

'Sorry,' Merri laughed, 'I'm getting carried away.'

'Sounds like we're both getting carried away — in different directions.'

'We'll keep in touch though, and more than cards at Christmas, goodness, we've been friends for three years.'

'Of course we will. And if I can get Robbie down that aisle, you're definitely coming to the wedding.'

'Try and stop me.'

★　★　★

First thing Monday morning, Merri drove into the nearby market town of Newark where she worked. Again, she was facing a situation she was not looking forward to, telling her boss she was handing in her notice.

'We're very sorry to be losing you,' Mr Markhampton, her immediate superior, said. 'Normally, of course, we should need a great deal more notice than just the one week but in view of your family circumstances and the urgency involved, we are quite prepared to waive this.'

But if her firm had been sorry, and were reluctant to say goodbye to her at the start of the day, by the end of the day, when she was back in Bingham again in the estate agents' office, they were only too delighted to greet her. They assured her that there would be absolutely no problem regarding the selling of number two, Tithbeck Lane. Apparently, it was a much sought after address.

Merri drove back to number two and began the mammoth task of packing. She had one week in which to do it but she was astounded at how much clutter she had accumulated since moving in. Pippa was similarly engaged and it was like a music hall farce as they kept on bumping into each other along the landing and hall both clutching bulging bags and cardboard boxes. Both new and exciting lives opening before them and it left precious little time for feeling sad at their fast approaching departure both from the house and each other.

On the last evening, Thursday, they were sitting in the kitchen having eaten a quick meal, knowing that it would be their last one together.

Merri said, 'If you can make use of any of the curtains, or for that matter, the carpets, Pippa, do say so, otherwise I'll just leave them in situ and the incoming people can decide what they want to do with them.'

'Thanks all the same, but they're really not much use to me because Robbie has his own house, you see, and it's already furnished.' Pippa reached for the last plate that was draining in the rack, dried it and spread the damp teacloth over the top rail. 'There, that's that.'

'Yes.'

They looked solemnly at each other. 'It's no good getting maudlin,' Pippa said.

'No point at all,' Merri agreed. 'We're both going to be doing what we want to do. It's the only way, isn't it?'

'Absolutely.'

'I shall miss you, you've been a really good friend.'

'Ditto to that.'

And then they were hugging each other tightly.

'Let this be one of our fond memories.' Merri said trying to hold back the threatening tears.

Pippa nodded. 'When we get in our eighties.'

And then they smiled at each other. It seemed a very long way off.

★　★　★

Immediately after work on Friday teatime, Merri drove straight from Newark to Bingham. Rather than disturb anything in the now pristine kitchen at number two, she opted to pop in to The Singing Kettle, the small cosy café in Bingham, and have a welcome cup of tea and an indulgent fancy cake oozing with cream — and calories. Fortified, she made her way to the library and returned her last three books, and wished the staff farewell. Then drove back to the house to load up the suitcases and boxes that were assembled and waiting in the hall. Finally, she turned the key in the lock and drove a seriously sagging Nelson down Tithbeck Lane and popped the keys through the estate agent's letter-box.

'Bridges fully burned,' she murmured softly as she started Nelson's engine and drove sedately through the square, past the Buttercross and out towards the double bend. As she did so, passing the church, she heard the bells begin to ring.

She smiled. They rang me in and they're ringing me out, she thought. Of course, it's Friday night, seven o'clock, bell-ringing practice.

It was a straightforward journey. Grantham was as quiet as a ghost town now rush-hour was over. Everybody was indoors, the streets deserted. She made very good time indeed along the almost empty main road heading further north into Lincolnshire and with a lift of spirits, spotted the signpost — South Rauceby — 2 miles.

'And here I come,' she murmured, swinging Nelson's wheel round with a flourish.

Prue was in the kitchen dishing up Bentley's food when Merri peeped through the window before tapping lightly at the back door. Bentley had been so engrossed in watching the knife chopping up the dog meat, saliva dripping from beneath dewlaps, it was a moment before he gave a warning woof, and even that was only a token one.

'Come in, darling.' Prue wrapped an arm around Merri's shoulders and squeezed her tightly. 'You're beautifully early.' In her other hand she waved the sharp knife. 'I'll just have to finish getting the dustbin's dinner ready or we shall have no peace, but it won't take long.'

'You carry on.' Merri dropped to her knees and made a fuss of the big dog. 'Fancy being called a dustbin. What a cheek isn't it, boy?' Bentley gave her cheek a long sloppy lick and resumed his single-minded stare at his dinner bowl.

'Stick the kettle on, Merri, we'll have a cuppa now you've arrived. The dinner's already in the oven, be about half-an-hour or more, okay?'

'Great.'

Whilst the kettle boiled, she slipped outside and removed all the suitcases and cardboard boxes from the stoic Nelson. Piling most of them in the hall, she took one suitcase upstairs to her bedroom. Pausing on the threshold and looking round, she gave a sigh of pleasure. Painted white with built-in wardrobes picked out in gold and a matching gold padded headboard above the white and gold sprigged throw-over on the single bed, the room was both soothing and welcoming.

Moving across to the window, she opened it and leaned her elbows on the broad sill. She looked out over peaceful pastureland to where the spire of North Rauceby's church was just visible peeping out above the tree tops. Far from being a sacrifice as Pippa had said, Merri knew it was in fact a blessing that she was here. Rafters felt like home. She could understand so well why her aunt loved this place. There was a special kind of magic at Rafters that wrapped itself around beguilingly, drawing her in and inviting her to stay. It was up to her to find a way to make the stables pay and ensure their future. Merri took one last deep breath of the clear fresh air and regretfully closed the window.

She flipped the catch on the suitcase and took out a long soft woollen skirt and powder-blue sweater. Quickly changing out of her severe black office suit, she consigned it to a hanger at the back of the wardrobe. Right now, it was totally redundant. From this point, her days would be spent dressed casually in jeans or jodhpurs and shirts that underlined the freedom of her new life style. But she knew it was a freedom coupled with commitment and hard work and resolved not to underestimate the mountain ahead that she had to climb.

'Merri,' Prue's voice called, 'I've just made a pot of tea. I'm taking the tray through to the sitting room.'

'Sorry, Prue, I'll be down right away.' Merri slipped on a pair of pumps, ran a comb through her hair and hastened downstairs.

Prue was just pouring tea. 'Help yourself to biscuits,' she said. 'I'm just going to put a match to the fire.'

'Why do I always feel so spoilt when you light a fire? Because I do. I think I might well be a frustrated arsonist underneath and it satisfies a basic desire.' She took her cup and sat on a low stool by the hearth.

'More likely it's a throwback to a primeval urge in the days when we all lived in caves. It was a symbol of safety then as well as a source of warmth and cheer.'

'I think you're absolutely right. It was a feeling I had straight away when I first arrived at Rafters, a beautiful feeling of safety.' She looked under her lashes at Prue, undecided whether to carry on and say what was in her heart.

Prue didn't look at Merri, simply smiled to herself and waited. Finally however, having decided her niece needed a little push, she prompted, 'I think you need to tell me the rest of it.'

Embarrassed now, Merri murmured, 'You gave me the feeling in the first place, way back, when I was only four. When you came into that room, picked me up and said, 'I'm taking you home with me.' They were the most wonderful words I ever heard. They made me feel warm, safe . . . just like the fire.'

As she finished speaking the intense stillness in the air eased as though the room itself, after holding its breath, had softly sighed, an almost tangible releasing of long ago deeply buried emotional tension.

'Now you know, darling,' Prue said, 'why I never regretted any past or lost opportunities. I've since been rewarded so very much. Caring for you was never a sacrifice.'

Merri was sorely tempted to tell Prue she had sold up the house in Bingham and was going to plough back the proceeds into Rafters and that to her was no sacrifice. But she intuitively knew Prue would forbid her to go ahead with the plan. So, instead, she reached for her aunt's cup and saucer. 'I think we could both do with a refill. And after that you stay exactly where you are and put the tootsies up while I dish up dinner.'

Prue smiled blissfully. 'That's a rare offer. I'm not used to being waited on and I'm certainly not going to argue.'

'Good.' Merri bent and kissed her cheek. 'I should think not.'

* ★ *

The alarm clock woke Merri at half-past six the next morning. Lying for a moment feeling disorientated as her sleepy gaze took in the unfamiliar surroundings, she remembered with a sudden rush of happiness this was to be her home now for the next few months. She recalled having been awakened in the night by the sound of rain being dashed against the windowpane by a howling wind. There was no sound of the wind now but hastily pushing back the covers, Merri padded over to draw back the curtains and see if the rain had stopped. Her first thought in the night had been what bad luck. Today was Saturday, the day of the village show. It would put a damper on the event, in more ways than one, if it was pouring down with rain. Outside the wind had dropped but it was still raining although not half so hard.

Drawing on dressing gown and thrusting her feet into furry slippers,

Merri opened her bedroom door. From the bathroom came the sound of water cascading as Prue splashed around in the shower.

Merri went downstairs to be greeted in the kitchen by Bently, who yawned and stretched extravagantly before licking her hand and taking up a stand by the back door. 'You make sure you're back quickly, it's not a day to linger. And don't even think about running off. I don't feel like chasing after you through the village in my nightie.' She unlocked the door and he nosed through impatiently. But she need not have worried, even before the kettle boiled he was back, shaking himself vigorously and spraying the kitchen with flying raindrops from his golden pelt. She fished in the roomy pocket of Prue's apron hanging behind the pantry door and tossed him a couple of dog biscuits. 'Now be a good dog whilst I take your mistress a lovely mug of tea to get her started.'

'You're a life-saver.' Prue reached

gratefully for the steaming mug. 'I think I'll pack you in my suitcase and take you with me to Dubai tomorrow afternoon.'

'Gosh, of course, it's Sunday tomorrow,' said Merri, her own mug arrested half-way to her lips. 'The time's galloping away now, isn't it?'

'Considering where we live,' gurgled Prue, 'that sounds about right.'

'So, this being our last full day together, what's the schedule?'

'We work in the stables as normal until twelve. Bed down the little beauties. Throw ourselves in the shower, have a bite to eat followed by putting on our best outfits and presenting ourselves down at the cricket field.'

'And where,' enquired Merri delicately, 'do we meet Matt?'

'Don't forget Walt,' Prue said archly.

'As if I could. I certainly wish I could, put it that way.'

'I'm sure you two will be fine when you get to know each other. Actually, Matt did hint that Walt's got, shall we say, a lot of baggage from the past. Of course he didn't say outright *what* it was, but he did infer that perhaps we shouldn't take Walt's bark too seriously, you know. We should make allowances.'

'Prue, Walt is a grown man and if he cannot carry his own baggage, it's a jolly poor show. I don't see he needs to inflict it upon everybody else.'

Prue smiled. 'I don't think he does. He saves it for you.'

★   ★   ★

It was just short of one o'clock when they hopped into Prue's Land Rover and she drove them down to where the show was being held. Even before they reached the cricket field, Merri could hear the distant strains of a brass band. They were belting out Colonel Bogey. She and Prue exchanged glances and giggled.

'I've a feeling we're going to enjoy ourselves this afternoon.' Prue bumped in through the wide open field gate and parked in the first available space in the field. They had barely got out and locked the vehicle before they spotted Matt and Walt coming towards them from out of the beer tent. 'Looks like they've made an early start,' said Prue.

'Hi, girls,' said Matt and threw an arm around each of them.

'Glad to see you made it,' Walt said. 'I hoped you wouldn't run into difficulties.'

There was a light-hearted gaiety in the air enhanced by the rows of brightly coloured bunting strung all around the ground. Merri decided she would not allow Walt's presence, or his comments, to spoil things. This would be the last outing she and Prue would have together for a long time and she meant to enjoy the day to the full.

Above the oompah of the brass band, stall-holders were doing their utmost to drum up custom. The vying cries of 'Roll a penny over here, folks', 'Try the coconut shy, gents, win a teddy bear for the lady', and from the rifle range,

'Three shots a pound', intermingled with the general hubbub of laughter and chatter from hundreds of happy people and no lesser amount of excitable children.

The four of them went on a leisurely jaunt around the perimeter taking in each attraction and stall. 'Guess the weight of the pig,' assaulted their ears and their noses confirmed it was indeed a real live one. 'Come along, girls,' the man in charge shouted zealously, his red hair as curly as the animal's tail, 'first prize is the pig,' and laughing, Prue waved aside the beckoning arm. 'I don't think I could cope with it if I won.'

They wandered happily round, with Prue doing the honours and introducing Merri to at least a dozen local people, including Janey's mum and dad, and being treated to ice-creams by Walt. They'd already sampled the hoopla, the coconut shy, guessed the number of pickled onions in the jar, had rolled lots of pennies down loads of shoots, when Prue suddenly grabbed Merri by the arm. 'Someone I want you to meet,' she said.

Over in the next roped-off corner, which in turn led through to a small paddock Merri could see five or six ponies, complete with a child in the saddle, plodding round in a large circle. Each had someone walking beside them holding a leading rein. On a straw bale to one side keeping one eye on the ponies and an even sharper one on the canvas bag of takings, sat an elderly woman sporting a straw hat. She was keeping time with the band by tapping one booted foot on an upturned bucket.

'It's Tabby, Mrs Carrier, you have to meet her,' Prue hissed, her fingers tightening their grip. She turned to the two men. 'We'll meet you two chaps in a couple of minutes, okay?'

'Anything you say,' agreed Matt.

'Are you sure it'll only be two minutes?' queried Walt. 'I don't think I'll bank on it.'

Stung by his comment, and springing to Prue's defence, Merri said, 'If my aunt said two, it will be two. Trust me.'

'I doubt I can,' he drawled, 'after all, you're a woman.'

Merri swung round and marched off, heading for the paddock, closely followed by Prue. 'Don't take any notice of Walt. You hit a nerve. He thinks women aren't to be trusted. Matt said so.'

'Tough. He needs to sort himself out.'

'Oh dear, and you were both getting on so well.'

'Hmmm . . . ' Merri said expressively, dodging through the straggling queue of excited children impatiently waiting their turn for a ride. 'Anyway,' she recovered her good humour, 'I'm not letting him spoil our day.'

They approached the old woman who ceased her toe-tapping and looked up as Prue said, 'Tabby, lovely to see you.'

'Well, you're a stranger, no mistake.

'Tis weeks since I saw you. Mind, that's how it is when you get a man. No time for anything else.'

'Oh come on now, Tabby, I've always had time for you.'

'Eh, get away, girl, I'm only leg-pulling.'

'Tabby, I want you to meet my niece, Merri. She's going to be running Rafters whilst I'm away in Dubai for a few months.'

'Is that so.' She frowned and scrutinised Merri closely. Then coming to a decision and nodding, she said, 'You'll do.'

'Will I?' Merri was nonplussed by the woman's uncompromising directness.

'She certainly will,' Prue beamed. 'I knew you'd like her, Tabby.'

'I do pride myself on being a good judge of people and horseflesh.' Whilst they were talking, Tabby was speedily relieving parents of the price of a ride, leaving the helpers to see the children safely on and off the ponies.

'They must be valuable ponies,'

Merri said. 'They look absolutely bomb-proof.'

'Indeed they are. Got to be d'y'see, they're used by the disabled riders.'

'Tabby runs Unicorn Stables over at Cranwell,' Prue said.

'Let's say I do up 'til this evening.'

'What?' Prue's mouth dropped open. 'You have to be kidding.'

'Anno Domini,' said Tabby. 'Can't go on forever.'

'But what will you do?'

'Retire, girl. Might still tell a few fortunes but that's about all.'

'Fortunes?' Merri queried.

'Tabby has second sight.'

'Have had since childhood,' agreed Tabby cheerfully, dropping another fifty-pence in the bag and watching the excited little boy swing a chubby leg over the pommel. She weighed the bag in her hand. 'Vicar's going to be right pleased with the takings.'

'And what about the harvest show?' said Prue. 'If you retire, who's going to organise the pony rides, then?'

Tabby smiled slyly. 'I could tell you but I won't.'

'Thanks a lot.'

'No offence, my dear, but I don't force the future's pace, even if I do know what will happen.'

'That's cryptic,' said Merri.

'Only for now.' Tabby handed her a business card complete with telephone number. And then she confounded them by saying, 'When you're ready, I shall be waiting.'

6

Bentley was whining. He'd been very restless for the past few days. It was a full week now since Prue had left for the airport.

'Take great care, darling.' Prue had held her very tightly. They were standing on the drive ready for leaving. 'Promise me something.'

'Yes?'

'If you find yourself up against it, please, please, promise me that you will go to Walt for help.'

Merri hesitated. She looked across to where Walt was sitting in the driving seat in the Range Rover. There was no possibility of him overhearing what they were talking about and she didn't want to upset Prue. There and then she decided her own petty opinion was of lesser importance than Prue's peace of mind. She swallowed the aversion she felt. 'Of course. If anything goes really drastically wrong, then yes, I shall call upon Walt.'

'Thanks. I was feeling so guilty, leaving you on your own, and now you've settled my mind.' At the words Merri felt relief. It was only a small thing after all and there was no way, she was sure, she would meet any situation that she could not handle herself.

When the Range Rover disappeared down the drive, Merri turned and went down to the stables. She stood in the middle of the yard. Everything was very quiet and she was aware of a great gulf of loneliness, something she had never experienced before.

These last few days had been a precious time. She had grown closer to Prue, discovered their true adult selves and developed a mature mutual love and friendship. Their relationship had moved on and developed. And now suddenly, Prue was gone. There was no doubt about it, she was going to miss Prue terribly.

For the following week she had been very busy running the stables and working eighteen hours out of twenty-four. Apart from the day to day physically exhausting work, there had been the additional workload each evening of trying to make sense of the paperwork which Prue in her usual haphazard fashion, had merely dropped into a box file. But by the end of the week it was all neatly filed, entered in the ledger and in order and Merri could begin to look forward, sure now of the path she wanted to take.

Late Friday afternoon the telephone rang whilst Merri was working down in the stables. She wiped her dusty palms down her jodhpurs and answered the extension in the tack room. It was from the estate agents in Bingham.

'Good news, Miss Williams, we have shown three prospective buyers over your property at 2 Tithbeck Lane and have just received a firm offer from one of them only £500 below the price you were asking. What would you like us to do?'

'Take it.' She could have danced with glee.

The time was already half-past four. Too late now for talking with the bank manager but next Monday she'd fix an appointment to discuss a loan. But what she had to do first, and pretty quickly, was put into operation a plan that she had begun formulating earlier in the week.

Digging Tabby's business card out of her jodhpur pocket where she'd thrust it for safe keeping, she dialled the number. It rang three times before Tabby answered.

'Hello, Mrs Carrier, it's Merri Williams here. Do you remember, we met on Saturday at the village show? My Aunt Prue from Rafters stables introduced us.'

'Of course I remember. I've been waiting for you to phone.'

'You have?'

'Oh yes.' It was said perfectly matter-of-factly. 'If you would like to come round to see me, this evening would be convenient. Say, in another couple of hours' time.'

'Oh, yes, yes thanks. That is what I was going to ask you. Thank you very much.'

'You'll have no trouble finding the stables, they're on Willow Lane.'

★　★　★

The Land Rover nosed its way up the bumpy driveway and Merri parked it at the side of the stable block. There was a light on in the kitchen window of the adjacent cottage and as she got out and locked the vehicle, she saw Tabby raise a hand in greeting through the window.

'Come in do. 'Tis nice to see you. Come on through to the sitting room we shall be more comfortable there.'

'Thanks.' Merri followed her and sat down in a rocking chair. There was a flurry from the bookshelf behind her and to her surprise, a Persian cat landed on her shoulder.

'Sorry about that,' Tabby said and

made to scoop up the cat.

'No, please, I quite like cats, she's fine.' The smoky grey Persian leaped delicately onto her lap and lying down, began purring contentedly. Merri stroked the long silky fur unsure now how to approach the subject of her visit. But Tabby sensed her awkwardness.

'You're here to offer to buy the ponies, aren't you?' she said in her usual forthright manner.

Merri raised her eyes in astonishment. 'Yes, how on earth did you know that?'

'Aah, I know lots of things.'

Merri smiled at her. 'Yes. I believe you do. Are you a witch?'

'Definitely.' Tabby grinned back. She pointed to the cat. 'That's my familiar.'

'Really.' Merri knew they were going to be friends.

'You want to buy them all, don't you?'

'Yes, but, er, it depends upon the price.'

Tabby named a figure that seemed

high but Merri knew to be consistent with the market price for expertly trained dependable ponies.

'I'll take them.'

Tabby rose. 'A small elderberry wine's in order, I think.'

'I'm driving.'

'Oho, it's not *that* powerful, and I'm only going to offer you one.'

'OK then.'

The subject of ponies was dropped as they went on to discuss Merri's arrival at Rafters and Prue's subsequent trip to Dubai.

It was the brass mantle-clock striking ten that abruptly interrupted their chatter.

'Heavens,' Merri said, 'I'd no idea it was as late as that. I must be going.' She tipped a most reluctant cat from her knee and held out her hand to Tabby. 'So nice to do business with you, Tabby. I'll sort out the stables, get them all prepared. Then, when I can pay you, I'll give you a ring and come over and fetch the ponies.'

'I think I can trust you. You come and fetch them Sunday afternoon, if you're ready.' Then added, slyly, 'It will save them eating their heads off here with me, especially now they're not doing any work.' They laughed.

'You're on,' said Merri, 'I'll be over.'

★   ★   ★

Bentley whined again, and scratched at the back door.

'You've been once already.' Merri let her spoon drop back into her bowl of cereal. She glanced at the clock. It was almost seven. 'I haven't time to come with you again now, I must get down the yard.'

Bentley scratched the door again.

'Oh very well, but just don't run off, right? And if you're more than a few minutes, you'll have to come and track me down at the stables.' He wagged his tail, a wide silly grin on his face as though he knew every word she said, and joyfully nosed his way out through the door into the back garden.

There was nobody else down at the stables. She'd asked Janey yesterday if she could do a few more hours overtime as well as the three she'd done on Saturday evening when they'd finally finished cobwebbing, sweeping, and scrubbing out six of the unused stables. It had been nine o'clock when they'd finished and both girls were exhausted. They'd left the six stable doors blocked open to dry off the wet floors. And now, this morning, Merri was going to put clean bedding down in each of them ready for the six new ponies they'd be fetching this afternoon.

It was only a few minutes drive from South Rauceby to Cranwell and Merri had asked Janey to be at Rafters by a quarter to two which would leave them time for several trips during the afternoon and the settling down of the new ponies well before early evening.

But Janey wasn't here this morning and Merri had all the seven original horses and ponies to muck-out, feed and water. It was well on into the morning before she finished the last one, slapped him on the hindquarters, left the stable and slid the bolts across before trudging wearily back to the cottage. She was beginning to realise just how demanding it must be for Prue running the stables on a shoestring with very little help.

Kicking off her boots in the back porch, she went through to the kitchen, flipped the switch on the electric kettle and slumped down on the kitchen chair. She was definitely in need of a strong coffee. But as she stirred the instant into a mug and added a full teaspoon of honey for a bit of go, she was aware of a sense of unease. There was something wrong, something missing. What was it?

She took the mug to the kitchen table and sat down again, taking a long sip of the reviving drink. And then it came to her — Bentley. Oh heck! That's what was wrong. Bentley was missing — literally missing. When had she last seen him? This morning as he scratched at the door? Yes, that was definitely the last time because she'd gone off to the stables, totally forgotten about him being let out and now it was obvious he had not come back.

She drank the coffee in quick urgent gulps, scalding her mouth, whilst her brain squirreled round madly. She had absolutely no idea where to begin looking for Bentley. But she had to find him, if not, however would she face Prue? Her aunt would be devastated.

Adding to her confusion, the doorbell rang, and carried on ringing, as though somebody had put their finger on the bell and was leaning on it. She banged down the mug, ran along the hall and tugged open the heavy front door.

'Yours, I think.' The voice was cutting as wind straight across a glacier. It was Walt. His eyes glittered like black ice. Thrusting forward his hand, he held out a piece of twine. Attached to the other end where it looped through his collar, was Bentley.

Relief turned her knees to water. 'Oh, Walt, you're an angel, you've found him. Thank you ever so much.'

'You are the most irresponsible, scatterbrained female I have ever been unfortunate enough to meet.'

Wrong-footed, Merri gaped at him. 'I beg your pardon? I'm really grateful to you Walt for returning him. I was so worried. Where did you find him?'

'I didn't, Janey did.'

'Janey?'

'He was in our tack room, shall we say, extending the paw of friendship to Gypsy. In fact, by the time I arrived, after Janey screamed for me, I found they were very, very friendly indeed.'

'You mean . . . ' Merri hesitated, feeling the colour rise in her cheeks.

'Yes,' he rasped, 'that is *exactly* what I mean.'

Merri gathered herself. 'Are you telling me that Gypsy's in season?'

'Of course she is. She was tied up in the tack room, which is why I'd thought it safe to leave the door open.'

'Oh dear.'

'Why on earth Prue left you in charge, I've no idea. You simply haven't a clue have you?'

Merri felt her temper start to rise. 'I thought he was missing Prue and that's why he was whining and restless.'

'Well, now you know it wasn't, don't you? You should have kept a closer eye on him.'

'We can all be wise afterwards, can't we?'

'Well, in future you keep to your patch and I'll keep to mine.'

'I certainly will.' Merri stuck her chin in the air and snatched the twine from his hand. 'I'm grateful to you for bringing Bentley back, thank you. I'll make sure he doesn't bother you again — and neither will I.'

Walt turned on his heel and strode away. Merri slammed the door closed behind him and went back to the kitchen. She was beginning to shake a little with reaction but Bentley, after slurping half the water from his bowl, took himself off under the kitchen table, lay down on his beanbag and fell asleep immediately.

Merri left him there and went outside. She was in need of some fresh air. She wandered round the corner, sat on the grassy mound at the base of the honey tree and leaned back against the sturdy firm trunk. It was comforting, supportive and the perfume from the blossoms soothed her jangled nerves.

She pondered over what Walt had said. How come it had been Janey who had found the dog? What on earth was Janey doing round at the livery stables at seven o'clock on a Sunday morning? She lived with her mother and father quite a few miles away and she didn't work for Matt at the weekends. Merri shook her head, it didn't make sense. Unless, the thought struck her, could it be that Walt and Janey were an item? The thought had a strangely depressing effect upon her. She supposed it was possible, after all that first day she'd arrived at South Rauceby and had accidentally skidded avoiding the cat, Walt had thought it was Janey who was driving. That indicated that he already knew Janey.

She closed her eyes and felt the warmth of the sun on her face and deliberately forced herself to relax and let the tensions within her melt away. What she had to concentrate on was Rafters' future. Anything else was irrelevant.

* * *

At a quarter to two Janey arrived in her old battered Metro. Merri had been waiting for her.

'Well now you're here, we'll get started straight away, shall we?'

'Sure.' She looked rather surprised. 'Is anything wrong.'

Merri locked the back door and climbed into the Land Rover. 'Wrong? No, why should there be?' She eased the Land Rover and the horse-box down the drive and out into the lane.

She deliberately didn't mention any-thing about Bentley or about Walt returning him. But Janey herself brought up the subject.

'I dare say Bentley's in need of a rest,' she said cheerfully, staring straight ahead through the windscreen.

'Yes.' Merri agreed. She didn't know what else to say.

'Did Walt tell you I found him in our tack room this morning?'

'Yes he did.'

Janey looked sideways at her, 'Oh, I see,' she said, and began to grin. 'You are putting two and two together, aren't you — and not just Bentley and Gypsy.' She giggled. 'And the answer to it, of course, is yes, I did stay the night there which is why I found him.'

'It's really none of my business,' said Merri, tight-lipped.

'All right, then if that's the way you want it.' Janey clammed up.

Merri wanted to scream, no it's not the way I want it. But instead, tightened her grip on the steering wheel, her knuckles now showing white, betraying the inner tension. She focussed all her attention on the road in front.

However, she had shaken herself by saying the words, albeit only within her head. But if that wasn't the way she wanted it, why not and which way did she want it? She found herself unwilling to answer those two questions. Walt had shown himself to be arrogant, self-opinionated and had warned her to stay away from him and that was exactly what she was going to do.

They drove on for a couple of miles in frosty silence.

Janey was the first to speak. 'Shall we begin again? Tabby's going to think it awfully strange when we get there if we're still not speaking.'

'Yes, she will, won't she?' agreed Merri, still smarting, but willing to accept the olive branch. 'Let's make it easier on ourselves as well, because we've a lot of work to get through, shipping all those six back.'

'Exactly.'

They drove on, but this time in a comfortable silence.

'If you don't mind my saying so,' said Janey, 'if you haven't already thought about it, you are going to be very hard pushed to cope all on your own. In fact, I'm sorry, Merri, but I don't think you'll manage.'

Merri bit her lip. 'Do you know,' she turned and grinned at Janey, 'the same thought had crossed my mind, too.' And suddenly they were back, friends once more.

Janey said, 'If I could make a suggestion, and I have to own up to a vested interest, I know a girl that would definitely, and desperately, be seeking work right now.'

'Do you?'

'Yup.'

'Stable work?'

'Oh, absolutely. Done nothing else since leaving school. Horses written all the way through like Skegness rock.'

'Go on then, who is she?'

'Eve, Eve Parsons. Lives at Cranwell.'

'Would she be someone I could rely on?'

'Gosh, yes, I can vouch for her.'

'And could she start straight away?'

'She's been out of work now for a week and, as you know, on stable wages you don't have much chance to save up a stocking-leg to fall back on if you are out of work.'

'Tell me about it,' said Merri, thinking of the figures in Prue's ledger.

They had reached Willow Lane in Cranwell and Merri swung the Land Rover up the bumpy drive into Tabby's stable-yard. Manoeuvring carefully, she turned the vehicle and trailer until she was pointing the way they had just come.

'Right, let's load up.'

Tabby had been hard at work and all six ponies were wearing head-collars and tethered to the rings in the yard.'

'Hi, Tabby,' she called, catching sight of the elderly woman just emerging from one of the stables. 'I'm all ready at the other end. Looks like it's going to take us three trips.'

'I'll need to speak to you when you've finished,' said Tabby coming across to them. 'But, it's a little bit delicate. How about you coming over later and having a bite of supper with me tonight? Both of you if you wish.'

Janey shook her head. 'Sorry, no can do. A meal with the parents tonight I'm afraid, very much Sunday duty and all that.' She laughed.

'What about you then?' Tabby looked at Merri.

'Certainly, thank you very much.'

'Half-past six do you?'

'Do me fine.'

'OK. I'll leave you to carry on and I'll see you then for supper.'

The trips back and forth between South Rauceby and Cranwell proved not to be as hard work as Merri had anticipated. The ponies were exceptionally docile and walked up the ramp into the horsebox without hesitation and were subsequently safely, and happily, installed in their new quarters with full hay nets to pull at.

The two girls stood in the stable yard well pleased with their efforts.

'And now it really does look like a working stable,' said Merri with satisfaction. All but one of the stables were now occupied.

'All you need now,' said Janey, 'is a lot more clients.'

★　★　★

Merri was thinking over Janey's words as she left Rafters at quarter-past six headed for Unicorn stables. It was just possible that Tabby could yet again prove the answer to her problem. If she had kept a list of her regular clients, she might be willing to accept payment for the goodwill and pass on the information, assuming, of course, she wouldn't be contravening the data protection law.

She knew there was a demand for horses to ride because during the week she had in fact had to turn down several prospective clients because she hadn't any horses or ponies available. But even though she had been forced to turn them down, she had kept a note of their names and phone numbers with the assurance that if they were prepared to wait a further week, she had more animals coming in and would be able to offer them a choice of rides.

Only this morning she'd received a call from a lady — a previously regular ciient of Tabby's — who had said Tabby herself had given her the number.

Merri was well aware just how much indebted she was to Tabby and with hindsight knew now why Prue had been so insistent that she should arrive at the stables in time to attend the village show on Saturday. By so doing, her aunt would be able to make the necessary introductions to ease her way. Without local contacts, she would have found it more than difficult to cope with running Rafters. Yes, Merri was very thankful for all the help she was receiving, particularly from Tabby and Janey.

It was a great pity that Walt wasn't similarly minded. She didn't want to make enemies, but it seemed, however inadvertently, that is now what Walt was. She'd promised Prue, and faithfully meant to keep that promise, that should anything drastic happen, she would call on Walt for help but she was going to make doubly sure that nothing did go horrendously wrong. There was absolutely no way she was going to crawl to him for assistance.

After parking in the Unicorn stable block, she went across to the cottage. There was a delicious smell of food coming from the kitchen and she realised the only thing she'd had since breakfast was the hastily gulped coffee prior to Bentley's return and since then she'd been far too busy to even think about food.

'Away and sit you down,' said Tabby, waving towards the sitting room. 'Do make yourself at home. Shift the cat if she's in your chair.' *Your chair*, thought Merri, hmmm, and went through and sat down in the rocking chair. This time there was no sign of the cat.

Tabby came through with two tiny glasses of elderberry wine. 'Here you are, my dear, this will give us both an appetite. It's a vegetarian dish, I hope that's all right? Lasagne?'

'Smells wonderful,' said Merri. 'I'm afraid I'm really going to do it justice. I've just realised I haven't had any lunch.'

Tabby laughed. 'Good job I've made an afters then.'

'You're spoiling me.'

'Well, whilst Prue's away I think I'll just appoint myself in her stead.' She kicked off her shoes and plumped down in the opposite chair. 'Do you want to bother talking business now or would you rather we had our food first?'

'Entirely up to you, I'm happy either way.'

'There's just one piece of business that I would like to sort out because it doesn't just affect me,' Tabby said, staring down into her wineglass. 'You see, it involves Eve.'

Merri's interest quickened. 'That wouldn't be Eve Parsons by any chance?'

'Yes. Do you know her?'

'No, but Janey mentioned her name, only this afternoon, actually. Said she was a friend of hers and mentioned that she'd been out of work for about a week and was desperately looking for another job.'

Tabby smiled. 'That's right. She is looking for another job. I've had to dispense with her services, as they say.' Then she grinned and added, 'But only because of my retirement.'

'Tell me about her. Janey didn't give me any details.

'Eve's been with me since leaving school and of course she knows each of the ponies personally, and all their little quirks.'

'I don't think they've got any quirks,' said Merri sipping the wine. 'They were some of the most well behaved ponies I've ever come across.'

'Well,' said Tabby, 'when I said quirks, I wasn't talking about misbehaviour but rather on the lines of which brand of peppermints they prefer, really.' They subsided into laughter.

'What do you think, then?' Tabby asked. 'You could do a lot worse. And if you are looking for somebody, I'd say she'd be the ideal person, wouldn't you?'

'Indeed I would. And I can't believe how fate is actually playing everything into my hands.'

'I shouldn't worry about that,' Tabby chuckled, 'it won't last.'

'I'm quite sure it won't,' Merri agreed.

7

'Miss Williams?' The query was coupled with a light tentative tap on the tack room door.

Merri looked up from polishing the length of rein she was holding to see a young fresh-faced girl with dark hair. 'Hi, you must be Eve.'

'Yes.'

'Come in, don't stand on ceremony, and the name's Merri, OK?' The girl nodded. Merri thrust aside the heap of tack she was cleaning and made room for Eve on the straw bale. 'Grab a pew. I was expecting you.'

'Can I help?'

Merri raised an eyebrow. 'Do you want to?'

'Sure.'

'In that case, cloths are over there,' she inclined her head. 'I understand from Janey you're looking for a job.'

'That's right.'

'And you were with Tabby Carrier, up until last week?'

'Yeah. I'm real sorry she's packed up but I suppose we've all got to retire at some time.'

Merri nodded applying saddlesoap to a pommel. 'Tabby's given me a glowing account of your work, and if you want the job, it's yours, but I can't pay you very much.'

The girl's eyes lit up. 'Wow, thanks very much. I'm not bothered so much about the money, I just need the job.' Then her eyes clouded over. 'I don't know if Tabby told you or not, but I actually, er — '

'Lodged with her?'

'Yeah.'

'So, you're looking for somewhere to live as well? Is that what you're trying to say?'

'Yeah, that's it.'

They rubbed away diligently at the dull leather bringing it back to gleaming life. Merri made a decision. 'I can offer you the room above the tack room here,' she looked up towards the ceiling. 'It's not very grand, in fact, it's as basic as it gets, but at least it's a roof over your head. Just the one main room really, with a bed-settee but there's a corner shower cubicle and separate toilet.'

'Sounds great to me.'

'You might not think so when you've seen it. But at least it's near to your ponies.'

'I love 'em to bits,' said Eve flourishing her cloth and polishing vigorously.

'I can understand that. They're some of the most well behaved ones I have ever come across.'

'Well, y'see, that's because they have to take disabled riders, some of the time anyway. They've got to be absolutely bomb-proof.'

'Yes, I was talking about that to Tabby. I was enquiring about the charity Riding for the Disabled but apparently Tabby wasn't in that. She'd just taken out additional insurance because apparently there are dozens of rules and regulations involved to become a member. Just one for example, you need a fully secured paddock to use and really, all I have is the gratuitous use of the forty-acre. Apart from that you've got to have adequate toilet facilities. So as things stand at the minute I don't think I'd qualify. In any case, it would all have to be inspected and would probably take weeks maybe even months, and I just don't have that sort of time in hand.'

Eve looked at her. 'Do you mind me asking why not?'

'I'm not the owner, that's my aunt, Prue Williams, and she's gone abroad for a few months. So, I'm only in charge until she comes back.'

'Oh, I see.' Eve pulled a face, 'It's a shame, I know a lot of our disabled riders are going to be real disappointed. It brightens their world up you know, being able to have a ride.'

Merri looked thoughtful, 'Yes, I'm

sure it does.' She remembered how she herself had felt taking that first ride on Crispin after a gap of three years. It did indeed instil a sense of freedom and well-being.

'They have to have helpers, to do lead reins and make sure they don't come a cropper, see? But they've all got their own friends, family, who are willing to help.'

Merri grinned. 'And you're saying I should take out this insurance and carry on where Tabby's left off?'

Eve grinned back. 'Why not?'

'Why not indeed. Even if I'm not a fully fledged member of Riding for the Disabled, I can do my bit to help. Except that I shall have to charge the normal rates, I can't do it for free. Otherwise we'd find ourselves charity cases.'

'That's brilliant,' said Eve. 'How are you going to let them know the ponies are here with you?'

'It seems Tabby's taken care of that because she had some enquiries from them when they knew she was closing down and she sent them all a letter explaining although Unicorn stables has now closed, they can ring me here, at Cornfields Stables. It's a good job I've taken you on the staff, isn't it?'

'Sure is.'

'So, here's your first official job. Since we're more than halfway through cleaning all this tack — could you make the tea, please?'

'Now that's the sort of job I like.'

They dragged the straw bale over to the tack room doorway and sat enjoying the late sunshine.

'Janey tells me you've been friends for years,' said Merri.

'Oh yeah, we were at school together. We go out to pubs, discos, that sort of thing. We were at the Dog & Duck over at Cranwell on Saturday night. She was a bit late meeting me 'cos she'd had to work some extra hours overtime. I didn't mind waiting, 'cos I got chatted up.'

'I thought Janey said there wasn't any

talent round here.'

'There isn't much,' admitted Eve. 'Except there's a gorgeous man taken over now at Chessington's, you know, Janey's boss? His name's Walt.'

To her chagrin, Merri felt her stomach flip over when she heard his name and was relieved that Eve was still prattling on.

'Anyway, this lad was still chatting me up, when Janey arrived. But of course she couldn't stay long — her parents are ever so straight-laced y'know.'

'Really.'

'Oh yes, she's got to be in by a certain time.'

'But she's over twenty-one.'

'Yes, but she's living in their house, isn't she? It's not like she can please herself, is it? I mean, parents still treat you like children.'

'Hmmm,' said Merri, noncommittally, wishing she had had the chance to grow up knowing her parents.

'Anyway, we had about an hour and

then decided since it was about quarter past ten, we'd make our way home. She has to be in by ten thirty.'

'You mean Janey went back to Sudbrook?'

'Yeah.'

Only Merri knew she hadn't done. Janey had already admitted she'd spent the night at Walt's.

★   ★   ★

Over the next two or three weeks, the stables were a whirl of activity with Eve moving in and all the new horses and ponies to integrate into the daily workload along with all the existing horses. But at the end of three weeks Merri sat down one evening to take stock.

She grimaced ruefully. She could fully understand now why Tabby had been only too pleased to let her have the horses and ponies rather than let them, as she'd put it, 'eat their heads off' at her stables. They were certainly busy eating their heads off now at Cornfields Stables. With sick disbelief she had noticed only that morning the stock of feed had dwindled alarmingly and she must immediately telephone for a large order from the suppliers. If not, she was going to be in real trouble.

The drawback to this however, was that the anticipated new clients from Tabby's existing clientele had not materialised. True enough, there had been several new enquiries that Merri had been only to pleased to oblige by supplying rides but they were far too few, and she had to admit it was very worrying. The amount of new clients needed to justify the purchase of the six extra animals and ensure the financial security of Cornfields Stables had in no way reached target.

And now also added to the additional cost of feeding, was the amount she also had to find each week to pay Eve's wages. But without Eve she wouldn't be able to cope with the workload. It was a vicious circle. And apart from the strictly business side of things, she felt the weight of moral responsibility. Not only did Eve rely upon her for a living but also for somewhere to live.

However, right now, stock needed to be fed. Merri knew she would have to dip into her own meagre savings to pay for a load of hay and horse nuts. But the little she had was not going to go very far at all. Most of her assets were tied up in the house at Bingham.

To add to her worries, the estate agent had telephoned that very afternoon to say the purchaser of 2 Tithbeck Lane had hit snags with the sale of their own property and were caught in a chain and an early signing of contracts could not now take place.

There was going to be no way she could repay Tabby in the foreseeable future and knew she would have to ring her this evening to let her know. She was not looking forward to it. Tabby had been her saviour and the thought of letting her down was unsavoury in the extreme.

Pouring over the ledger, Merri knew that she was in an even worse situation at Rafters now than when she'd arrived. Her stomach contracted against the thought that maybe despite all her best intentions and efforts to pull Prue out of the mire, she had merely thrust them both further in. What she desperately needed was an influx of clients. But knowing what was needed was one thing — how to attract them was quite another.

Feeling on the verge of panic, she pulled herself up sharply, and thought of the old adage. You have to speculate to accumulate. And although there was precious little to speculate with, Merri was certain that was what she must do. However short of cash she was at the moment, there was no alternative but to keep on ploughing it back into the business. She had to get it on a secure footing. Prue had a very good reputation and Merri was sure if people were only made aware of the wider choice of rides available, they would begin to patronise Cornfields Stables.

She had enquired about the cost of additional insurance for taking on disabled riders and had been horrified at the amount. But if she did take out the cover, it would broaden her client base considerably, she knew that. Without the insurance, that potential group of clients was lost. Tabby had included in the price of the ponies all the necessary specialist tack that was needed which meant no further expense would be incurred.

But in addition to targeting those particular clients, she also needed to attract new ones. And that meant advertising. The local newspaper would obviously be the first choice but she also needed to have flyers placed in the local shops for a radius of about ten miles. Once the advertisements were in place the one thing to do then was dig in and keep going, whatever the cost, and wait for the phone to start ringing.

Things looked pretty tough right now but there was no other option than to keep going. And as the mountain, rather than diminishing with all her hard efforts, seemed ever to rise higher before her, Merri knew her own determination to succeed must also rise to meet the challenge.

Laying aside her pen, she went through to the kitchen and began to make coffee. Bentley, who had been full-fed and asleep on his beanbag under the table contentedly snorting, suddenly twitched and woke up, nose scenting the air. He gave a short warning woof and as if on cue, there was a ring at the front door.

Merri glanced at the wall clock, it was getting late and she was not expecting callers. She snapped her fingers and called him to heel. Rafters was far enough away from the nearest property for her to feel quite isolated although normally, this wouldn't bother her at all, but most legitimate callers would have come during daylight hours — now it was almost dark. However, with Bentley by her side she felt quite safe. Switching on the outside light, she opened the front door. There was a man standing there. It was Walt.

Merri was completely taken aback. He was the last person she'd expected to see. Bentley recognised him and cavorted around excitedly.

'Hello, Merri. I'm sorry to be calling so late in the evening, but I've only just finished work. Do you think I could come in for a minute, please?'

Merri took a deep breath, her stomach had yet again, and much to her annoyance, done a back flip. 'I thought,' she said frostily, 'you told me to stick to my patch and you were going to stick to yours. Well, this *is* my patch and I'm sticking to it. Where does that leave you?'

He smiled crookedly, 'Infiltrating?'

Merri took a step backwards. 'I suppose if you insist on coming in, you'd better,' she said ungraciously.

'Oh I'm not insisting, but I would very much like to. I don't feel like apologising to you on the doorstep.'

'What? You want to apologise to me? I don't believe it.'

'I really think it would be better if we didn't discuss this on the doorstep.'

'Then, please, do come in.' She turned and walked down the hall. Bentley, stern waving, followed behind Walt. Going into the kitchen, Merri swung round to face him.

'So, just what is this apology?'

'First of all, let me say I'm sorry I doubted your word.'

'And which word would that be?' She was determined not to make it easy for him.

'When you first arrived, after you drove Prue's horsebox into the ditch.'

'Excuse me,' Merri said coldly, 'I did not drive into the ditch, I skidded.'

'Yes, OK, you skidded.' He held a palm up placatingly. 'You told me you'd been avoiding a cat.'

'Which was true.'

'As I now know.'

'Oh. Well, it's taken you long enough, several weeks actually, to acknowledge I was telling you the truth. I'd hardly call it a blinding flash of illumination.'

'That's because it wasn't,' he said bluntly. 'I only found out an hour ago.'

Merri stared at him before reaching for a second mug out of the cupboard.

'I was about to make coffee when you rang the bell. I think I'd better do it now whilst you explain.'

He smiled. 'I think that would be an excellent idea.'

Merri made coffee with hands that were slightly unsteady. The force of his smile in the confined area of the kitchen was lethal — and she was shaken to find she wasn't immune.

'I really am sorry, Merri. At the time I had no idea who you were and I was just concerned about Prue.'

'And Janey.' Merri couldn't help adding it.

'Yes, OK, and Janey.'

'All right,' she said grudgingly, 'I can understand that. You'd never seen me before and you were just looking out for them both.'

'That's right.'

'So what happened an hour ago that has changed your mind about me?'

He looked at her very directly. 'I was in our tack room an hour ago and the cat walked in.'

Merri frowned. 'It could have been any cat. How do you know it was that particular one?'

'Because it fitted your description and it was also carrying this.' He unfastened his puffa jacket and very gently slid a hand inside and withdrew a ginger kitten wrapped in a thick towel.

Merri stared. 'But . . . whose cat is it?'

'You're not going to believe this,' Walt said. 'It's Matt's. Her name's Smitty. She went missing a few weeks ago and he was convinced she'd gone away to have a litter of kittens in secret. Smitty was a stray that he adopted about six months ago. Matt reckoned her previous owners must have destroyed a litter she'd had and this time she was simply making sure they'd be safe.'

Bentley was sniffing around most interestedly. He ruffled his nose through the tiny kitten's fur and jumped back only just in time as the little orange bundle spat ferociously and struck out with a tiny needle-sharp claw.

They laughed out loud. Both knew the ice between them was melting.

'I appreciate your coming to apologise and I accept it, but what are you going to do about the kitten?'

'We . . . ell,' he drawled, 'I was thinking . . . maybe you'd like it?'

She leaned against the worktop and looked at him. 'For someone who said I hadn't got a clue about looking after stock, that's going it a bit, don't you think?'

'Perhaps I was a bit hasty,' he said. 'Mind you, you'll have to make sure you keep it in. At the moment it's pretty feral. Come to think about it, perhaps I'm not doing you any favours. It's going to take quite a bit of taming.'

'But the mother cat belongs to Matt.

Won't he want it?'

Walt grinned. 'Well considering Madam Smitty proceeded to walk in with three more, I'd say Matt will have sufficient, wouldn't you?'

★   ★   ★

'It's a good job I didn't go in for a career in sales,' Merri said to Bentley, throwing herself down into an easy chair and kicking off her shoes. She stretched her toes and wiggled them luxuriously. 'It's harder work than mucking-out.' Bentley leaned against her leg, placed his muzzle on her knee, looked at her with deep soulful eyes and sighed with the air of a martyr. 'Now what's the matter with you?' He looked up at her and then rolled his eyes expressively towards the window. Merri followed his gaze. 'Oh, I see.'

She pushed him gently away and walked across the room to where the long red velvet curtains hung from ceiling to floor by the french windows.

Two-thirds of the way up, clinging on desperately, fur standing on end and a wild gleam in his eyes, the kitten eyed her. She reached up to unhook him and the kitten struck out with a sharp claw raking the back of her hand and drawing blood. But it was his undoing. Unbalanced now, he waved a paw desperately, trying to regain a grip on the curtain and in so doing, began to slip. Merri stepped forward and swiftly grabbed the scruff of his neck. She set him down kicking and squalling furiously on the carpet.

The minute she released her hold he flew underneath the music centre and she could hear him swearing to himself. Getting down on hands and knees she began, in honeyed tones, to try and coax him out. But his reaction was merely to fluff out his fur, back away into the corner and jam his little bottom firmly against the skirting board.

Merri retreated to the kitchen and returned with several small chunks of cheese. She lay full length on the floor and proffered the first one. It took a lot of patience but at the end of ten minutes the kitten had eaten every bit. 'I don't think you're as wild as you're making out. I think it's because you're frightened of me, timid.' She sat back on her heels. 'I can't keep on calling you kitten and because you are timid, I'm going to call you Timothy. But it needs to be a bit grander than that, doesn't it? How about, Timothy Whiskers? What do you think?' She bent down again to look at the kitten. There was no sign now of the miniature tiger — he looked adorable, sitting up on his back legs and washing his face and whiskers with both front paws. Merri smiled and said softly, 'I'll take that as a yes.' At least, she thought, I'm making progress with this little chap. All it takes is trust.

She collapsed once more in the easy chair. It had been an exhausting afternoon. After placing the eye-catching advertisement in the local newspaper, she had driven around in a wide radius of ever decreasing circles around South Rauceby. At every shop and possible advertising outlet, she had called in and tried to persuade them that putting her flyer in a prominent position so their customers couldn't help but see it, was their number one priority. It had been very much a case of some you win and some you lose and her nerves were feeling pretty shredded but at the same time she knew that widely advertising Cornfields Stables was the only way to awaken awareness in possible future clients.

Since Walt's visit a week ago she had felt that perhaps they could, after all, be friends and had in fact accepted his invitation to go for a drink at the local pub, albeit for only an hour at lunchtime. They had skirted warily around each other, both unsure how far the truce extended. But they had parted amicably and to be honest, Merri had thoroughly enjoyed his company and was looking forward to seeing him again. She had not thought any further about the night Janey had stayed over, had almost forgotten about it — until this afternoon.

At the end of her long trail around the local villages, and with only one flyer left, had gone into the shop in Sudbrook. The bell had tinkled discreetly as she pushed open the door and went down the one step inside. The woman behind the counter smiled at her as she approached.

'I wonder if you could help me?' Merri held out the advertising flyer. 'Would it be possible, please, for you to display this in a prominent position? I don't mind paying for it. Shall we say for the following month?'

The woman glanced at the wording and then looked up with a smile of recognition. 'You're Prue Williams' niece, aren't you? From Rafters.'

'How on earth did you know that?'

'Can't you remember me? Your aunt introduced us, at South Rauceby show. I'm Janey's mum, Muriel Pemberton.'

'Of course.' Merri extended her hand. 'I'm so sorry, Prue introduced me to such a lot of people that day and it all became a blur. I do beg your pardon.'

'How're things going over there?'

Merri pursed her lips a little. 'We could do with some more clients.'

Muriel nodded. 'Like business every-where. And talking of work, thank you for keeping Janey on at the stables and also for giving her the chance of a few hours overtime a short while ago. It all helps. And we weren't worried after she rang and said because it had got so late, she was spending the night with her friend, Eve, over at Cranwell. A nice girl, Eve. A suitable friend for Janey.'

Stunned, Merri managed to say. 'Janey's a very good worker.'

But it had been on her mind all the way back from Sudbrook. She could hardly believe that Janey would lie to her parents like that.

Now, lying back in the easy chair she thought about Muriel's words. All her old animosity towards Walt resurfaced. Could it be he had put Janey up to lying to her parents to cover himself? Merri desperately hoped not. She felt very confused.

But, analysing her feelings honestly, she was forced to admit, that despite the animosity, she also found Walt extremely attractive — that there was chemistry between them couldn't be denied. They had only to look at each other and high-voltage electricity zipped from one to the other. The current was so strong as to be almost tangible. She would be all sorts of a fool to deny it. And intuitively, Merri knew Walt was certainly very much aware of it himself.

But one thing was clear, she needed to find out the truth before their relationship could progress any further. She had to be sure that Walt was a man she could trust.

8

It was working.

She'd been right to go ahead and invest in the advertising even if the eye-catching ones in the newspaper were costing far more than she had anticipated. The phone was continually ringing now with enquiries, her list of clients expanding most satisfactorily and this morning she had had the papers through from the insurance company confirming she was now fully covered if she wished to take on disabled riders. And she certainly did. Indeed, having expended the cost of the insurance, it was vital she recover the cost back again. And all this before Cornfields Stables began to show anything in the way of profit. But things were looking good and she was beginning to feel hopeful about the stables becoming a truly viable business.

She had a list on her desk of enquiries from disabled persons who had previously had riding lessons with Tabby and this evening she intended to ring round as many as possible and start booking in. It was essential that she stressed they must each bring two helpers — there was no way she wanted to run any risks whatsoever with their physical wellbeing. Any chance of a fall had to be minimised. She shuddered at the thought of the cataclysmic results a fall would have on their existing disabilities. But before she could begin to ring each of the people on the list, there was the present working day in front. Glancing at her watch, Merri hastily swapped her working shirt for a clean sweatshirt emblazoned with Cornfields Stables. No way was she going to let Prue down by appearing to be running the stables in a sloppy manner. Reputation was all-important.

It was only four weeks since the advertisements had been put in the newspaper but, checking out all the rides booked for this morning, she was gratified to see that one ride included eight horses and a second an unbelievable thirteen. Thirteen was the maximum they could accommodate at any one time and that meant instead of having a ride herself, she would be cycling alongside instructing and advising. It was looking good. She mentally gave herself the thumbs up and decided to treat herself at lunchtime.

She hadn't seen anything further of Walt but she had thought about him a great deal. When they'd looked across the kitchen at each other, laughing at the kitten's antics, electricity had positively crackled between them. And she had to admit, despite the unpleasant undertone regarding Janey having admitted spending the night at the livery stables, she really missed Walt and wanted to see him again. Perhaps after all it had been quite innocent and she was reading far too much into it. It would be a great pity to allow it to spoil any possible blossoming relationship.

Thinking again of his smile she knew by her involuntary emotional response, he attracted her as no other man had ever done. And she deserved the chance of a fulfilling joyful relationship — it was something every person had an automatic birthright to, the precious sharing of life with one special person.

She had worked very hard to reach this point and now it looked as if success was on the way and she felt quite justified in allowing herself to stand back a little from the business and think about her own personal needs — and exactly what *they* were.

Making up her mind, she decided after the last ride had returned to the stables and the horses were bedded down with full hay and water, she would drive over to Chessington's and ask Walt if he would like to go to the local pub for a lunch time drink. Having taking the decision, she felt a rise of excitement, the morning was going to seem far too long before it reached midday.

There was nobody around in the stable yard when she parked the Land Rover. Obviously, their morning session had ended much earlier than her own. She crossed the yard to the back door of the house. The door stood ajar a little and she tapped on it and called out his name. Immediately, there was a crescendo of barks and a whirlwind of snowy curls and ringlets exploded across the kitchen. Walt had not exaggerated the affectionate nature of his Labradoodle. Gypsy licked her furiously, jumping up and down in an ecstasy of greeting.

'She remembers you,' said a familiar voice.

Merri felt a tingle run through her. 'You can certainly rely on dogs. They always give you a welcome, whatever.'

'And you can't say that about men?'

'I think that would be going it a bit. However,' she smiled at him, acutely aware, particularly now after an absence of several weeks, of the force of his magnetism. Magnetism was the only word — she felt powerless to resist. She bent over fussing Gypsy to hide the fact her cheeks had coloured. 'I thought maybe you and I could go down to the pub and have a little liquid refreshment? It's been a long hard morning.'

'Sounds to me like a good idea. Give me one second to get the keys and some cash and I'm with you.'

They didn't bother to take the vehicle but leisurely wandered down together through the village. It was very hot and both opted to take their drinks out to the back and sit in the shade of a tree in the beer garden.

Merri suddenly felt rather shy. It was all very well being a modern woman and asking a man out but, somehow, it seemed rather forward and she was glad there were several other people sitting outside enjoying their drinks in the sunshine. She glanced at her watch. 'I can only stay half an hour.'

Sensing her slight withdrawal, Walt said, 'This is precisely the reason I haven't got in touch before. It's not that

I don't want to spend time with you, Merri, believe me, I really do want to, a great deal of time. I just didn't want to force the pace.'

'I'd thought you might ring or perhaps drop in.'

'Did you want me to?'

'I hoped you would.'

'Good.' He sighed with satisfaction and took a gulp of the cold beer. 'That's all I needed to know.'

Merri sipped her fruit juice. It was all very well Walt taking it as read their relationship could now move forward, until she had the answer to what was bothering her so much, it was still stalemate as far as she was concerned. But how to raise the subject was tricky.

'How's the kitten?' he asked.

'Timothy Whiskers? He's fine.'

'That's his name is it?'

'Hmmm, it seemed to suit him. He didn't seem to be really wild, more very timid. He just needed to learn to trust me.'

'That's all it takes, trust?'

She looked at him. 'It surely is.'

He took another gulp of his beer. 'Perhaps I should try it.'

'Perhaps we both need to.'

'Don't you trust me, Merri?'

'I'd really like to.'

'So, what's stopping you?'

Now was the moment. She knew she wouldn't get such a God-given perfect opportunity again.

'I need — '

'Hi both. Wow, do I need a cold drink.' Eve had walked round the corner carrying a misted glass of shandy. 'Mind if I join you?'

Merri didn't know how Walt felt but she could have strangled Eve right then. Instead, she swallowed her annoyance and said, 'I believe you know Walt.'

'Yeah.' Eve looked at him seductively under her lashes. 'But we've not been formally introduced.' She shot a right hand across the table almost spilling his beer. 'I'm real pleased to meet you.'

'Likewise,' said Walt, laconically,

rescuing his drink and leaning back in his chair.

Eve prattled on happily and presently Walt began to beat a soft tattoo on the table top with his fingers. He finished his beer. He and Merri exchanged glances.

'This reminds me of Brief Encounter,' said Merri.

'I was thinking exactly the same,' he replied.

'I've heard of that,' chipped in Eve. 'It's an old black and white, isn't it?'

Walt nodded, not looking at her.

'I suppose you could call it that, couldn't you?' she smiled at them. 'I mean, we're only here very briefly and I've just encountered you.'

'That's true,' said Merri, but couldn't meet Walt's eyes.

Abruptly he stood up. 'Anyone fancy another drink? I'm going to go and fetch one.'

Merri looked at her watch mindful of the next booking at Cornfields. 'I don't think I will, Walt, if you don't mind. I've still some left.'

'Oooh, yes, please. I'll have another, if you're offering.' Eve drained the remains of her shandy and pushed it across to him.

'Righto.' He took the empty glasses and went back into the pub.

'Oh wow.' Eve's gaze followed him. 'Has he got pulling power or what? And don't you think it's just too sexy, that limp of his? You know, like one of those cowboys, sort of rolling a bit when they walk.' Merri didn't answer. Undaunted, Eve continued, 'Well, anyway, I do, I think it's dead sexy. I could go a real bundle on him.'

'Could you now.' Merri played with her glass, twisting the slender stem around in her fingers. 'But don't you think he'd be a little too old for you?'

'No way. Mature, that's what he is, experienced.'

Despite herself, Merri couldn't help smiling, 'Get away with you. He's not going to start cradle-snatching is he?'

'He might.'

But at that moment their conversation ended because Walt reappeared with a couple of glasses.

'We could all do this more often, couldn't we?' said Eve happily, lowering the level in her glass.

'I don't think so,' drawled Walt. 'It's not something I'd want to make a habit of, lunch time drinking.'

'Oh.' Eve thought a moment, 'Tell you what, we could do it after work, when we've finished for the day. It'd be great. What do you think?'

'Count me out,' said Merri. 'I'm sorry, but my day doesn't finish when the stable closes. I'm usually busy on the books after that.'

'Well, what about you then, Walt?' From being momentarily downcast, she perked up again.

'Sorry. No can do. Like Merri, my day doesn't end there either. It's called the joys of being the boss.'

'Anyway,' Merri finished her drink and stood up. 'I'm sorry but I really must get back.' She looked across at

Eve who finished her shandy.

'That means me too. But I've enjoyed the brief encounter.'

'Guess I'll just stay and finish my beer then. Bye girls.'

Merri walked back out into the pub car park. Eve climbed into her ancient Mini. 'Where's your car then?'

'I've left mine at the livery stables. You carry on, I'll see you back at Cornfields.'

'OK.' Eve shot off leaving behind a cloud of exhaust fumes hovering in the hot summer air.

Walt materialised at Merri's side. 'I'm afraid that screwed everything up.'

'Never mind.' They walked back down the dusty lane to Chessington's. As she was about to start the Land Rover engine, Walt leaned in through the open window.

'I didn't want to make a threesome but how about you and me making up a twosome at some point? We could have a drink or a meal, whatever you like.'

'I'd love to.'

'Great. We can start working on a little thing called trust.' His face softened to a tender smile and her heart did a back flip. 'I'll give you a call, we'll fix something up.'

'Could you make it after next week though, Walt? I've a tremendous workload.'

'Business booming?'

'Just beginning to take off, yes.'

'That should please Prue. By the way, have you heard from her? I got a letter from Matt about a week ago.'

'Only a postcard. That was a few days after she left saying she'd arrived safely and she'd write as soon as she got the chance.'

He nodded thoughtfully, 'I just thought I'd ask.' His face through the window was very close to her own and she understood only too well what Eve meant by pulling power. Despite her lingering doubts, his attraction was so powerful it drew her to him even against her better judgement.

He reached in through the open

window and removed her hand from the steering wheel. Keeping his eyes fixed on hers, he lifted her fingers and softly brushed his lips against them. Merri felt a charge of electricity tingle through her whole body. However much she might try and hold him at arm's length until she'd eradicated the lingering doubts, deep down inside she knew she was falling in love with Walt. Intuitively, she knew they were playing out some preordained destiny. Whether that destiny would end in happiness or tears she had no idea, only the Gods themselves knew.

However having driven back to Rafters, she chided herself for being fanciful. The all-important question still remained unanswered. The way forward between them was still blocked.

It was not something she could come right out with and ask Janey without risking provoking her and possibly ruining a very good working relationship. And she was not prepared to take the risk. The workload, as she had told

Walt, was tremendous and it would be a total disaster if Janey walked out right now.

The last of the chores finished that evening, Merri sighed with relief. A long soak in a hot bath filled with fragrant bubbles would be heaven. She went upstairs accompanied by Timothy Whiskers. He scampered in front into the bedroom. Sitting down on the stool in front of the mirror, she unclipped a pair of tiny pearl earrings. As she reached out towards Prue's jewellery box on the glass-topped dressing table, the kitten, thinking it was a game, lunged forward and skittered on the slippery surface. He cannoned into the jewellery box and knocked it flying. The box struck a corner of the solid wood chest of drawers and the impact jerked it apart.

'Oh no . . . ' Merri fell on her knees and gently lifted it up off the floor. But it was not broken as she feared. The blow had merely released a shallow drawer from underneath which she had never noticed before. Inside was something wrapped in tissue paper. Merri carefully removed the wrapping. As the last sheet of tissue paper fluttered free, she could see it had concealed a photograph. It was a photograph of Prue as a young woman — and she was holding a baby.

Merri turned the photograph over. There was a date written on the back, 1974, followed by the words: 'My darling Ella'. She sat and stared at it. Who on earth did the baby belong to? She had never heard Prue mention any child by the name of Ella.

In the photograph Prue looked about seventeen or eighteen. But it was the way she was looking at the baby, the expression on her face, tender, loving — almost maternal.

Deeply disturbed, Merri slid the secret drawer back into the jewellery box and replaced it on the dressing table. Taking the photograph with her, she went through to the bathroom, ran the bath hot and deep and poured in a generous helping of bubble bath. She propped the photograph up between the soap-dish and the tiled surround, climbed into the bath, lay back and stared at it. It brought home to her again what sacrifices Prue must have made in her youth, having to deny herself a child of her own through looking after Merri. Because that was what the expression on her aunt's face showed, the love of a mother for a baby.

An hour later she was downstairs wrapped in a towelling bathrobe and sipping a hot drink. But she was no nearer finding a solution. She still had absolutely no idea of why Prue should have hidden the photograph inside the secret drawer in the jewellery box. It was not an action that would have been taken lightly. It had been the only thing in the drawer — which made the photograph significant. And that being so, the baby must also be of enormous importance.

She sighed, shaking her head, it was a baffling mystery. But, one thing was sure, when she next spoke to Prue, she would certainly ask her.

Despite it being still only early evening, she felt exhausted and couldn't be bothered to get dressed. Her head ached abysmally. But she had set herself the target of ringing round the list of disabled people that was waiting on her desk. Knowing she couldn't relax in any case, she finished her drink and went over to the desk, lifted the telephone and dialled the first person's name.

Out of the eight names listed, she managed to contact six. They'd all, without exception, greeted her call with delight and immediately booked in for rides. Merri replaced the receiver after the last one and made an asterisk against the two who were not at home. She'd try them again tomorrow.

Strangely enough, her headache had lifted. She had enjoyed talking to each of them and it had taken her mind away from her own problems. It put everything firmly into perspective when she considered what they themselves were coping with daily and, possibly, for the rest of their lives. Her only regret was that she had to charge them a fee. There was absolutely no way round it, certainly not at the moment. But at least she was offering them the chance of a little enjoyment and it had lifted her own spirits to know that she was helping them, even if only in a small way

Considerably more cheerful, she rang Tabby to share the good news.

'Hi Tabby, it's Merri. Just ringing to let you know from tomorrow your ponies will be giving rides to people who'll really appreciate them.' Tabby's reaction was gratifying.

'Merri, my dear, I can't tell you how pleased I am. It was an awful wrench when I had to admit that my old bones were getting old and it was time I hung up my riding boots. But it was not a decision I made easily. I knew if I hung up my boots they'd be doing the same and it wasn't a comfortable thought. So I am very pleased to hand the reins over to you.' They both laughed.

On impulse, Merri said, 'Tabby, I know you and Prue were close, can I ask you something? Did Prue ever mention to you a baby, or possibly a child, called Ella?' Was it her imagination, did the line give a slight hiss or did Tabby catch her breath? 'Tabby? Are you still there?'

'Yes, I'm still here. And I did hear what you said, Merri. I'm afraid I cannot tell you. You must ask Prue. I am sorry.'

'Have you been sworn to secrecy?'

'That is an unfair question, my dear.'

'I think you've answered my question. Well, part of it. As to who Ella is you can't tell me, can you?'

'No, I'm sorry. The only thing I can say is, ask Prue.'

★ ★ ★

Wilma's plump face split into a wide grin of joy as she walked down the stable yard with her mother and elder sister. She looked at each of the ponies in turn and then gurgled with delight and threw her arms around Snowball. It was one of the ponies from Tabby's yard.

'Got a thing about that pony,' said her mum to Merri. 'Comes alive when she's near him.' And indeed, the child, who had Down's Syndrome, was chattering away joyfully, rubbing her hand up and down his muzzle.

Merri felt a tight knot at the back of her throat as the child, supported on either side by her family, climbed up onto the pony's back. The animal stood rock-steady. Janey gently clucked and led him forward on the leading rein. Seeing the bliss on the little girl's face, Merri knew she had taken the right decision. The money now was immaterial, this was something that needed to be done, a service that had to be given.

And when Julian, another child with Down's Syndrome, arrived a few minutes later, his reaction was almost identical to Wilma's. But his favourite was Pandora, a sweet-natured bay pony that stretched her neck towards him and whickered softly in recognition.

Merri met Janey's eyes, which were bright with unshed tears, as were her own, and knew it was not just herself who was fighting down pity. Intuitively, she realised it was misplaced pity. It was not wanted. The children were more than happy. Their expectations of life were simple. They extracted joy from each moment undaunted, unaware of their grave disabilities. But as Merri quelled her feelings of pity, she allowed herself to be moved by compassion and silently vowed she would do everything she possibly could to keep Cornfields afloat.

Both children were excited at being in the saddle again, but Merri insisted, as she led Julian's pony, that they kept to a walk even after they had clip-clopped their way down the lane and entered the forty-acre. Their safety was absolutely paramount and although she had checked out the doctors' certificates that stated they were eligible to ride, she was taking no chances.

Initial experiences were so important and she was determined that nothing should mar this, their first outing with Cornfields Stables. To begin with, she would need to assess their riding capabilities. To be doubly sure, she made a mental note to have a word with Tabby to see what degree of riding expertise each disabled rider already possessed.

But the children were just so happy to be seated astride the ponies again, feeling the exhilaration of freedom of movement after the enforced break from riding, they didn't bother about going any faster.

It was a scorching hot day with just light wisps of delicate cloud crossing the wide sweep of blue sky. Merri was very relieved that today had turned out to be a glorious day when it could easily have been pouring down. The only drawback to this, as evidenced by the ponies' swishing tails, was that the flies were out in force and determinedly hovering around their heads. She made a further mental note to get some fringed, fly-repellent brow bands for them.

They did a complete circuit around the perimeter of the forty-acre and after closing the gate behind them, clip-clopped back up the sunlit lane to the stables.

When the children had finally left, enthusiastically blowing kisses from the cars' windows, Eve pounced upon Merri and Janey.

'How'd it go? Everything OK?'

'It went very well,' said Merri. 'And thanks, Eve, because I'm so glad you made me think really hard about doing this. It's so worthwhile.'

'The look on those children's faces,' said Janey, 'it wrung my heart. You don't realise, do you, being non-disabled, just how fortunate you are and what problems other people have to cope with?'

'Very true,' Merri agreed. 'Anyway, now we've started, I'm absolutely one hundred percent behind this venture. I intend to keep it going.'

'Yeah.' Eve punched a fist in the air.

★ ★ ★

The next few days were a whirlwind of activity and Merri was busier than she had ever been in her life before, fitting in as many of the disabled riders as it was possible to do within the existing framework of rides for the non-disabled riders.

Even with Eve's help, and Janey working part-time, the workload was truly staggering. Each night she'd barely energy enough left to eat a meal and have a quick bath before falling exhausted into bed.

But it was worth it, at last the stables were paying their way. All she needed now was for the estate agents to ring and say they'd sold her property and she'd be able to repay Tabby. It was the one thing she felt really bad about, although Tabby had repeatedly reassured her she didn't mind waiting.

It was not until the following weekend that Merri realised that she had not received a telephone call from Walt. It was well over a week now since he had promised, but then, she had asked him to back-off whilst she got herself through the initial sorting out period. However, she was feeling more than ready to take a breather from the demanding schedule and wise enough to know she not only needed one but would work all the better afterwards.

She decided that at the end of the week, if she still had not heard from Walt, she'd pop up to Chessington's and surprise him, possibly arrange for them to go out for a meal on Friday evening.

The rest of the week slipped by in a blur of activity and it was Friday before she realised it. But having completed the last of the rides that afternoon, she told Eve to take charge. She was going to give herself an hour off.

It was yet another glorious day and rather than take the Land Rover, Merri decided she couldn't be bothered driving, she'd slip round to Chessington's on the bicycle. It was very pleasant skimming along the narrow leafy lanes their grass verges awash with daisies, golden dandelions, and tall, peppery-smelling cow parsley. Her spirits were high as the wide blue sky above as she turned into the livery stable yard. It was going to be a wonderful evening — just the two of them together.

Coming to a halt, she saw Janey emerge from the tack room and raised a hand and was about to shout a greeting. Then, she froze. Walt came out right behind her and, slipping an arm around her waist, pulled Janey close to him. Even as Merri watched in horrified disbelief, Janey raised her face to his and Walt bent his head and kissed her.

Backing away, hurt beyond belief, Merri silently turned the bicycle around and fled.

9

The airmail letter lay on the mat inside the front door. The postman had delivered early this morning. Merri, clutching a throbbing head and with eyes gritty from lack of sleep, stepped carefully down the last tread of the staircase, crossed the hall and bent to pick it up. The act of stooping instantly made her head hurt even more. She turned the thin envelope over. The sender's name and address was written right at the bottom. It was from Prue in Dubai. Despite the hollow misery inside her, Merri began to feel marginally better.

She went outside. Although it was still early, the sun had already been up for a couple of hours and was increasing in warmth all the time. It was going to be another scorcher. Merri walked round the cottage corner and sat down on the grassy mound and leaned against what she now perceived to be the one truly permanent support in her life. The honey tree bark felt warm against her shoulder blades as she leaned back and wriggled herself a comfortable spot. The flowers with their perfume had long since withered away but the comfort the tree always brought her remained constant.

The tree was like a true friend, always there, available to listen to her troubles and in its silence and support she found her own strength. It was strange, because after all, it was only a tree but it symbolised so much more to Merri. It was the one place she had instinctively sought out yesterday when she had returned from Chessington's livery stable. She hadn't uttered a sound but merely thrown herself down under its shady, silent protection. She was totally devastated and too numb to do anything else. And it had only been Eve calling her name that had roused her.

Reluctantly opening her eyes she'd

looked at her watch. With a shock she realised Eve should have knocked off over an hour ago. Scrambling to her feet, Merri took a deep shuddering breath and gathered herself. It was totally unforgivable of her to have left Eve on her own all this time.

She thanked her and apologised, said goodbye, and went down to the stables. Having checked everything was in order and that the horses and ponies were secure for the night, Merri returned to Rafters.

As she entered the kitchen her gaze fell on the beanbag beneath the table. Normally, it was Bentley's own private domain however this evening it was not just the dog that was curled up blissfully fast asleep. Snuggled between Bentley's paws, also fast asleep, with his little ginger face pressed tightly up against the dog's muzzle was an equally blissful Timothy Whiskers.

Merri just stood and looked at them. It was the first time they'd both allowed the barriers to fall exposing their vulnerability, and going to sleep together. As her heart warmed at the sight of them, Merri felt the stunned numbness wearing off and hot tears began to trickle down her cheeks.

The next moment she fell on her knees beside the beanbag and gathered them into her arms and sobbed and sobbed. Timothy Whiskers, with rank disapproval, struggled from beneath her arms, tail twitching in annoyance and leapt up onto the cushion on the kitchen chair. But Bentley, empathising as only a dog can, remained where he was, gently thumping the beanbag with his thick golden tail and soulfully licking the tears as they trickled down her face.

It wasn't the fact Walt obviously preferred Janey to her that hurt so much but rather, he had betrayed the trust she'd only just felt secure in giving to him. Now it was shattered into tiny fragments. If the experience wasn't to colour the rest of her relationships in the future, she had to learn to trust again. Not Walt himself, she knew she could not trust him a second time, but for her own salvation, Merri knew she had to be strong.

Now this morning's letter from Dubai had begun the healing process. Her heart and spirits had begun to lift. Wriggling back into a more comfortable position against the ridges of the honey tree's warm bark, Merri slit open the letter. It was quite short and the overall tone was sombre.

Dear Merri, Do you remember how I began the letter I sent to you way back in May? There is never a right time . . . my darling, this again appears to be holding true for me out here in Dubai. I know now I have left it too late. I should have made the effort a long time ago but I'm a coward, like the rest of us, and I kept putting it off. But God in his wisdom has allowed me a little grace and I have had two months saved from the wreckage of a lifetime and for that I am eternally grateful.

I cannot at this moment be more

specific, my darling, I wish I could but I want to tell you the truth myself, face to face. The situation here can have only one outcome and accordingly, when I have dealt with everything, I shall be returning home to Rafters very much earlier than anticipated, probably within the next week or two. Until then, all my love, God bless, Prue.

Merri stared at the lines of handwriting. Whatever her own troubles here in England, it would seem that over there in Dubai, Prue was coping with something of far greater importance.

In reflective mood, she took herself down to the stables and starting on the end one, began automatically mucking-out.

The pony in this stable was Chequers, possibly the ugliest little pony Merri had ever seen. He was a skewbald, blotched irregularly in brown and white with a mane that definitely did its own thing whichever way you tried to lay it when brushing and would split and lie in untidy hunks either side of his neck whilst his forelock stuck out like a veranda. His conformation was anything but copybook: short in the leg, long in the neck and with a dished face. And because of his age, his lower lip hung loosely showing his long yellowed teeth. But if his appearance was ugly, his temperament was beautiful. And she had no need to tie him up whilst she went about putting in fresh bedding and refilling his hay net and water. Dipping into her pocket, she palmed him a mint. 'Good boy, Chequers.'

It was not always appearance that counted.

At half-past seven Merri heard Janey's old car pull into the stable yard. A few seconds later she appeared at the stable door.

'Morning, Merri.'

Merri, bent double cleaning out Crispin's hooves with a hoof pick, was grateful for the fact that she needn't look directly at Janey. Wishing her a good morning in return, she fought down the unwelcome feeling of jealousy at the thought of Janey and Walt together. It was no good letting personal feelings ruin a working relationship between herself and Janey.

It was going to be a testing morning. The first ride out at nine o'clock comprised of six disabled children. There was no way she wanted to antagonise Janey. She knew she had to rely upon her to help run the stables and the bottom line was, the stables came first and her personal feelings second.

A few minutes to nine, the disabled riders and their helpers began to congregate in the yard. This morning she had two new clients. One, a little girl called Lucy who she knew from speaking to her mother previously over the phone, had been blind since birth and who was six years old. The other was a little boy, Harry. He'd had a deformed left knee since birth and wore callipers. Harry was four years old. Altogether there were several disabled children riding out this morning.

Merri offered up a prayer of thanks. She wouldn't have time to dwell on her own petty problems, she would have to keep her attention fully focussed on their needs.

Delegating Janey and Eve to look after the four regular riders, Merri took charge of Lucy and Harry. With each of the other four children, she had not asked which pony they wanted but had merely allowed them to go down the line of stables until they'd found the one they were looking for. It had always worked very well before and the children were overjoyed at finding their particular equine friend themselves.

In Lucy's case, Merri experienced a qualm at just how she was going to accomplish this because Lucy was totally blind. However, she allowed Lucy, clutching tightly to her mother's hand, to go down the line of ponies. The little girl ran her hands over the horses' muzzles and around their heads to begin with, then on down their necks and withers ending with fore legs.

She checked out and passed over two ponies that had been designated 'their' ponies by Wilma and Julian and Merri breathed a sigh of relief. A dispute over who was to ride one particular pony she could do without. Then Lucy examined a third and there was not a single flicker of reaction. But, impatiently now, tossing back her coppery ringlets, she approached the fourth pony, which was Chequers. The minute her small hands traced the contours of his muzzle and lower face, it was as though a lamp had been lit inside her and she squealed with delight. Flinging her arms around his neck, she patted along the dishevelled line of his shaggy mane, crooning to him.

'I'll leave you to make friends again,' Merri, moved by the child's happiness, squeezed Lucy's arm gently. 'I'm just going to talk to Harry for a few moments and then I'll come back.' But Lucy wasn't listening. She was far too busy rekindling friendship with Chequers who seemed equally pleased to see her.

Harry stood in the middle of the stable yard looking round with enormous grey eyes and a big smile on his face. His two helpers were elderly ladies who each held one of his hands.

Merri walked over and hunkered down in front of him. 'Hello, Harry. Can you tell me which pony you'd like to ride?' Overcome by sudden shyness, he stared hard at the ground and simply nodded. 'Do you know his name?' Merri prompted.

'Yes.' It was little above a whisper. 'Mr Chips, please.' Then, daringly, he looked up into her face with huge, expressive eyes, and treated her to a gorgeous smile. 'Please.'

'Come along, then. Let's go and find him.' The ladies released their hold on the child and Harry trustingly transferred his grasp to Merri's hand. They walked at an erratic pace, accommodating the restrictions of Harry's disabled leg that was encased in a calliper. But when he caught sight of the fat little Palomino, he gave a shrill cry of delight and tugged his hand free. Scuttling awkwardly but at amazingly fast speed to where the pony was tethered, Harry flung himself upon Mr Chips.

Meantime, Merri waited for Harry's two lady helpers to catch up with her. She had originally spoken to Harry's father on the telephone when he had booked the little boy in for rides and she was interested in finding out who they were. One of them held out the requisite doctor's certificate. Merri read it through quickly and handed it back.

'I'm Megs Atkinson,' she said and motioning to her companion, 'this is my sister, Beatrice.'

'Pleased to meet you.' Beatrice shook hands with Merri.

'We're both so pleased you've taken over where Mrs Carrier left off,' Megs continued. 'We live next door to Harry but his father very often asks us to baby sit and rather than us going to Harry's, Mr Mitchell brings Harry round to our house. Actually, he often stays over-night.'

'Obviously he trusts you implicitly with Harry,' Merri said.

'Well, he and his wife go out quite a lot, you see,' explained Megs.

'And we love having Harry,' Beatrice said. 'In fact, we sometimes have him for a week or more when his parents go away on skiing holidays.'

'I see.' Merri smiled and nodded. 'It must be very nice for you both.' But inside, her heart bled for the little boy and she silently formed her own private opinion of Harry's parents. She looked across the yard. The child was stroking Mr Chip's shoulder, patting gently and talking to the flicked forward ear that told Merri the Shetland pony was listening to what Harry was busily telling him.

'I'll go and pop Lucy into the saddle on Chequers,' she told the Misses Atkinsons, 'and then I'll come back and we'll have Harry up on Mr Chips. Perhaps you would help me to remove his calliper.' Her eyes swept down to professionally assess his surgical boot and, judging the width of it, knew that the normal stirrup iron would accommodate it safely.

Lucy was still busily chirruping away to Chequers and Merri softly interrupted her. 'We're ready to ride out now, Lucy, would you like to mount?'

'Yes, please,' Lucy immediately ran her hand down Chequer's neck to his withers, turned to face his tail and reached up ready for the reins. Merry put them into her left hand and she leaned against his neck for support. Then, with a helper either side for safety, Merri placed the child's left foot into the stirrup.

'Ready, Lucy?' The child nodded. 'Right. A little spring and put your toe down.' But Lucy didn't need any prompting, she knew what was required. And a second later, she'd swung her right leg across the saddle and was sitting securely astride. Reaching down, she felt for the leathers for her right leg and slid her foot into the iron.

Merri turned to her mother. 'It seems

Lucy can ride, but I'm afraid we have to keep the pony on a leading rein in her case, I'm so sorry.' She said it in a low voice so the child didn't hear. But Lucy's mother nodded. 'Yes, I know, it's quite all right. Lucy's just so happy to be on the pony, she's not bothered about being allowed to ride solely on her own.' Merri sighed with relief. Although the children all had their own particular disabilities that created some problems, for the most part, they were much easier to deal with than some of her able-bodied riders who were sometimes extremely picky.

Returning to Harry, Merri led Mr Chips over to the mounting block and the Misses Atkinson sat Harry down on the lower step and with the skill of familiarity, swiftly unbuckled the calliper and released the velcro straps allowing the calliper to unhinge and be lifted off Harry's leg. The little boy obediently waited until Merri told him to lean across the saddle and whilst Beatrice Atkinson walked round to the right-hand side to prevent him slipping, Merri lifted Harry's right leg over and Beatrice guided his foot into the stirrup. Megs slid him into the saddle, guiding his left leg into position. A beaming smile on his face, Harry gathered up the reins like a professional and Merri quickly ran the leathers up higher until the iron was level with his ankle bone and then gently slid his surgical boot safely into the stirrup. And throughout, Mr Chips stood like a statue.

Merri quickly checked the rest of the riders and found, as expected, because she had now come to rely, with gratitude, upon Eve and Janey's expertise, everything was in order. All the indispensable helpers had taken hold of the leading rein to each pony and were waiting to pull out.

'All ready?' she called.

And everybody was.

'OK.' Merri quickly mounted Crispin, 'Let's ride.'

And to a chorus of excited whoops

from the children, they set off.

She led the string of ponies out of the stable yard and down the lane to the forty-acre. The atmosphere was light-hearted and the children's laughter and obvious pleasure was reward enough for all the hard work. Merri allowed four of the children who were really quite competent riders to trot but, of necessity, Lucy was restricted to a walk and although she suspected that Harry was also a good rider, this being his first time at Cornfields, he too was only allowed to walk his pony. But each of the children was in high spirits and it was not hard work supervising them, rather, a fun experience to be enjoyed with them.

It was very hot and although the ponies had been fitted with special brow bands and sprayed with fly repellent down their necks, there were lots of flies about. But the perfectly schooled ponies took the minor irritations in their stride and apart from a lot of ear twitching and the occasional shaking of the head, behaved impeccably.

The ride, having covered over half the distance around the perimeter of the forty-acre, were headed back when Merri noticed a familiar figure leaning on the hinged end of the gate watching them. It was Tabby.

'You'll have to forgive me,' she said, twinkling up at Merri as they approached, 'I had to come and see their happy faces now they're riding again.' She waved an encompassing hand towards the six children whose shrill voices and laughter seemed to expand and fill the field with a joyful and tremendously positive energy.

Merri twisted in the saddle and leaned back supporting herself with a hand on Crispin's warm back. She scanned the little group, well pleased with their progress. 'Plucky kids, Tabby. They teach us, not the other way round.'

'Couldn't agree more,' said Tabby cheerfully. She raised a hand in greeting as the children recognised her. 'You've my new one, I see. The little boy on Mr Chips.'

'Yes, Harry.'

Tabby dropped her voice. 'I feel a bit sorry for the little chap. His parents live in Cranwell but they never bring him, always send him with Megs and Beatrice. Don't think they bother a great deal about him.'

'My impression too,' Merri murmured. 'But he seems happy enough on the pony.'

'Keen as mustard,' Tabby nodded. 'I gather Harry really kicked up about being allowed to ride and it's only recently his parents have finally given in.'

'P'raps they were being protective because of his disability.'

'Hmmm,' Tabby sniffed expressively, 'Beatrice told me they'd said they didn't want him going down *that* road.'

'Meaning?'

'Not sure, but they certainly don't like horses.'

'Well, their son doesn't take after

221

them.' They were watching as Harry had cajoled Janey into leading Mr Chips around in a big circle. His grin was pure Cheshire cat.

'Anyway,' Tabby unhitched herself from the gate. 'Must be off. I'll pop round again.'

'Do, anytime, bye.'

The hour had passed very quickly and all the children were disappointed now it was time to return to the stables.

'Never mind,' she commiserated as they dismounted in the stable yard. 'You are all booked in next Saturday morning.' There was a chorus of delighted agreement.

★　★　★

At half-past six with the working day now behind her, Merri returned to Rafters and after feeding Bentley and Timothy Whiskers, thankfully stripped off her jodhpurs and working top and climbed into a soothing hot bath. It had been a long tiring day. When she considered it, she realised she'd slept very little the previous night and had begun work at the crack of dawn. It was no wonder she was exhausted.

But it had been worth it. For the whole of the day she hadn't thought once of Walt. She'd been far to engrossed in work. Now, with the lonely evening stretching away in front of her, her thoughts returned to the previous day and the scene she had witnessed.

It was so difficult with Janey working side by side with her, that Merri could see no alternative other than to pretend she had not seen her with Walt in order to maintain the smooth running of the stables. But she acknowledged she was putting herself second and self-worth was not being acknowledged. Just how long could she continue to do so before damaging her own self respect?

But half an hour later, dressed in clean jeans and cotton top and drinking a reviving mug of tea in the kitchen, the telephone rang. It was Walt. His first words threw her.

'Do you want to speak to me?'

Merri's heart began thudding uncomfortably. Could it be that Walt himself had actually seen *her* on the bicycle at Chessington's? Stalling, she said, 'Why do you ask?'

'Well I promised to ring you after a week and it's a lot longer than that.'

At least, that means he doesn't know I witnessed him coming out of the tack room with Janey, thought Merri, which also means my dignity is still intact.

'Do you forgive me? Merri . . . are you still there?'

Collecting her scattered thoughts, she said, 'Yes, I'm still here and I think it would be better if we didn't see each other again.'

'I beg your pardon?'

'Oh I think you heard what I said.'

'I heard, but I don't understand.' There was a sharp edge now to his voice. 'What is it I'm supposed to have done?'

'I think you know. I don't have to spell things out.'

'You've lost me. I've no idea what you're talking about. However, there's something I definitely want you to see here, at the livery stables. I was ringing to see if you'd like to come over this evening and I'll cook a meal for us both.'

Merri could barely contain her rising anger. 'I don't think it's me you should be saying this to, do you?'

There was a short silence and then he said, 'If the mountain won't, Mohammed must.' And the phone went dead.

Merri hoped she had misunderstood what he had said. Tired and hungry, a visitor was the last thing she wanted this evening, particularly Walt. She decided if he did have the effrontery to ring the doorbell, she would simply not answer it. Having decided that, she set about preparing her evening meal.

The fish had almost finished grilling and the salad had been prepared when there was a blast on the front doorbell. She jumped, then straightening her shoulders determinedly, continued laying out the cutlery. The doorbell continued to ring — incessantly. But now Bentley, casting bewildered glances first at her and then looking towards the door began to bark. The fish was done and Merri slid it from under the grill onto her plate and set it on the table. Bentley, by now, was beside himself, barking continuously and she bent down and ruffled his ears. 'It's all right, boy. I know who it is. I can hear the doorbell but I don't want to see him.'

'Well, I'm sorry to disappoint you,' said a familiar voice behind her in the kitchen doorway, 'but you're going to.'

Merri gasped and spun round. Walt, having decided there was no point continuing to ring the bell had walked round the corner and entered through the wide open back door. Bentley bounded over, tail sweeping from side to side, licking the man's hand furiously, whilst above his head, Walt and Merri glared at each other.

'Since you appear to know something

detrimental to me that I don't, perhaps you wouldn't mind sharing it,' he said and went over and leaned against the sink unit. He waved a hand casually towards the table. 'Your meal's getting cold.'

Merri was tempted to pick up the plate and throw it at him. 'Your barefaced cheek leaves me speechless,' she said.

'Not good enough. I'm still waiting to find out what I'm supposed to have done.'

'OK.' Merri was trembling with barely controlled anger. 'I saw you. I actually came to your stables yesterday afternoon to invite you to have dinner with me that evening and I saw you.'

The annoyance left his face and he looked bewildered. 'But what was I doing?'

'You were coming out of the tack room — with Janey. Do I have to say more?' A slow smile replaced bewilderment on his face. 'You didn't hear me,' she persisted, 'because I didn't come in the vehicle, I came on the bicycle.'

His smile broadened and he nodded his head. 'I get it. You saw me kiss Janey, right?'

She clenched her hands, feeling the nails biting into the palms. 'Yes.'

He threw back his head and laughed.

'How dare you . . . '

'Oh you silly, silly girl.' He was across the room in two strides, pinning her arms to her sides with his own and his lips crushing hers.

Struggling violently, she managed to free one hand and delivered a stinging slap across his cheek. But even that didn't stop him. He reached out and caught hold of her hand before she could repeat it. There was a dark red weal beginning to show across his cheek and she knew it must be hurting because her palm was stinging like mad. He totally ignored it however and marched her out of the kitchen, stopping only to turn the key in the back door, and bundled her into the Range Rover.

'Just what do you think you're trying

to do?' Merri put a hand on the door handle. 'I'm getting out of here.'

'No you're not,' he said, chuckling, and his hand closed over hers preventing her escape whilst with the other hand he turned on the engine. Selecting first gear, he set off. Once the vehicle was in motion, Merri knew it was hopeless to try and get out and she sat simmering all the way down the lanes until they reached North Rauceby. He was still chuckling as they swung into Chessington's yard then, turning towards her said, 'Come with me, there is something you have to see.'

'Nice try, but I'm walking straight back home.' She swung open the door and leaped out.

'Oh no you're not.' He ran round to her side of the vehicle and grabbed her wrist. 'Come on. You're coming over to the tack room. You have to see this.'

He was far stronger than she was and after an initial futile struggle, Merri gave up and allowed herself to be taken into the tack room.

'The reason you saw me with Janey was because she had spent all afternoon in here with me.'

'I don't want to hear all these . . . sordid details.' She spat the last two words at him.

Abruptly, he released his hold and frowned. 'There are no sordid details. Look,' he pointed to the far corner under the big bench. There was a big cardboard box containing a thick blanket and inside Merri could see Gypsy curled up, her eyes watchful, somewhat wary. Walt bent down and passed a hand over her head. 'It's all right, girl,' he said, 'it's all right.' Then he dropped his hand, picked something up and brought it over to show Merri. 'See,' he said.

It was a day old puppy.

'Oh,' Merri gasped, 'it's gorgeous.'

'And you have a vested interest in this litter.'

'I do?'

'Bentley, of course, is the father.'

Merri's eyes widened as she looked first at him and then down at the wriggling puppy. 'Of course, that Sunday he got out.'

'Yes,' Walt nodded, 'but you and I have got over that. What you have to get over now is what you saw yesterday.'

It was Merri's turn now to be wrong-footed and bewildered. 'Please, explain it to me.'

'When you arrived here yesterday the vet had left only a few minutes before. Gypsy had a rough time and I had to call him in but Janey was here, helping me. Janey and I had just been out and burned all the whelping newspapers and we'd returned for a last look at the puppies before going to make a much needed cup of tea. What you saw was me, delighted that Gypsy was going to be fine and the puppies were all safe too, giving Janey a big thank you kiss for all her help. Because, believe me, she was a big help.'

As the last of her anger drained away, Merri felt swamped with relief. Walt, watching her face, seemed to know how she was feeling.

'It's all to do with that little thing called trust, isn't it?' he said gently, his eyes now soft, warm, as he looked at her. And Merri nodded. Their gaze met and held. The puppy in Walt's hands whimpered shrilly and he bent and replaced the little creature with its mother.

Straightening up, he took Merri in his arms, cupped her face between his palms and looked deep into her eyes. 'Let's not have any more misunderstandings between us, my darling. Do you think we could try again?' he said huskily.

Merri reached up and stroked his cheek, 'Yes, please,' she said in a low voice.

Bending his head, he gave her a long, tender, kiss.

★　★　★

It was not until she was back at Rafters, very much later, that Merri realised she still did not know the truth about what had happened when Janey spent the night with Walt.

10

'Chessington's Livery.'

'Walt, it's Merri.'

'Darling, something wrong?'

'I have to speak to you, now. Not over the phone, though.'

'But it's nearly eleven, won't it wait until tomorrow? I mean,' Walt chuckled, 'I should hate to ruin your reputation.'

Merri thought about Janey and winced. 'You said no more misunderstandings between us, didn't you?'

'And there is one?'

'Yes. I did mean to ask you earlier but I forgot.'

'Ask away.'

'I can't, not over the phone. Please, Walt, can I come round?'

'No.' His voice was firm. 'Stay there, I'm coming over.'

Within minutes he'd arrived and was seated in an armchair in the sitting room. Merri had spent those few minutes dreading what she thought would be a possibly disastrous confrontation. But she herself couldn't remain seated and began padding up and down, searching desperately for the right opening.

Walt watched her for a moment or two and then said, 'Well, for someone whose supposed to be running Prue's business efficiently, you're scoring a home goal.'

Merri stood still and looked at him questioningly.

'The carpet.' He smiled at her, 'You're wearing it right through. Prue will need a new one.'

'I don't know how to put this,' Merri began.

'Jump in.' He leaned back in the armchair folding his arms across his chest.

So Merri jumped.

Walt listened impassively as she explained exactly what was bothering her. Merri found when she reached the end that her hands had clenched themselves and her heart was thudding away as though she'd just run up a hill. 'So, please, I want the truth.' She sat down suddenly as her knees went weak.

He simply sat and stared at her. 'Have you ever wondered why I kept Janey on at the livery stables?'

Merri, having steeled herself for the worst was thrown by his question. 'What has that to do with what I've just asked you?'

'A lot.'

'Well, go on.'

'I know Janey was employed by Matt before I came here. But with the amount of workload over at Chessington's, I could handle it by myself.' He smiled wryly. 'Jockeys are used to long hours and hard work.'

'So?'

'If I had released Janey from her duties, that would have left her in an intolerable situation.'

Merri, eyes wide now wondering

what was coming next, listened without interrupting.

'What I'm trying to say, Merri, is that I personally do not need Janey, but the fact is, Janey needs me.'

Merri felt the rise of anger within her. Walt saw the red flush rise up her cheeks and hastened on. 'I don't mean she wants me, as a man. I mean, from the employment side.'

'But you're not a charity.' Merri found herself interrupting, waspishly.

'No, I'm not. But when Matt returns he will need help but in the meantime it would mean a great deal of hardship to Janey to lose her job. And the reason for that,' he swept on, seeing her mouth open as she was about to speak, 'is that her father is fighting cancer of the liver.'

Merri was stunned. She had had no idea.

'He is too ill to work,' Walt went on, 'and I am not going to add to Janey's problems by pitching her out. Do you understand?' Merri nodded. And he continued, 'She was very grateful to you for giving her several hours' overtime that Saturday evening but because she was late leaving work, it made her late in turn getting to the pub at Cranwell where she'd arranged to meet Eve. But where things really went wrong was, after having had a drink with Eve, Janey found her car was not as reliable as she'd hoped and it broke down on the road towards North Rauceby. There was no hope of her getting home to Sudbrook.

'Janey walked into Chessington's very late that evening. She had left her car by the side of the road and she asked me to see if I could get it to start. However, I couldn't. It's so old it really wants dumping at the scrap yard. But because it was getting so late, Janey was getting very distressed about getting home to her parents. I don't know if you're aware of it but her parents are extremely strict.'

'I do, actually,' Merri said in a low voice, 'Eve told me.'

'The last thing that Janey wants right

now is to upset her father in any way.'

'Yes, I can understand that.'

'So, at my suggestion, she telephoned her mother and said she'd had to work late, which was true, and she was spending the night at Eve's. A white lie, yes, but I think in this case, justifiable.'

'And she spent the night with you?'

'Correction. Janey spent the night at Chessington's — in the guest room.'

They stared at each other.

'Thank you, Walt.'

'What for?'

'For feeling you could trust me enough to tell me.' And suddenly the atmosphere lightened and they were both smiling now.

Walt glanced at his watch. 'It's getting late. I really think I should be going.' He grinned. 'Don't want the neighbours thinking Prue's cottage is a place of ill-repute.'

'Oh, talking of Prue,' Merri said, 'before you go, there's something I'd like you to read. You were asking if I'd heard from her and she's sent me a letter.' She retrieved it from behind a brass candlestick on the mantelpiece where she'd hastily filed it.

Walt read it through quickly and then a second time more slowly. 'She doesn't give much away. Any ideas what she means?'

'None whatsoever. Except that it sounds as though she'll be coming home at very short notice.'

'It also looks as though you may have to prepare yourself for something of a shock.'

'Maybe. But I'm hoping Prue won't get a shock when she gets back, because I have made some sweeping changes.'

'Have you?'

'Yes. For a start, I've bought in six more ponies.'

'My word.' His eyebrows shot up. 'A costly business.'

'I've also taken out additional insurance to cover myself.' She thought of the children's faces that morning alight with pleasure and felt a surge of happiness. She caught hold of his hand, wanting to share it with him. 'Oh, Walt, it's something so worthwhile. I only wish I could do it without charging, but I can't. Well, certainly not yet, anyway. I didn't want to tell you until it was successful.'

'What are you talking about?'

'I'm giving rides now to disabled people. Isn't that fantastic?' Her enthusiasm and eagerness were brimming over.

His reply was a bombshell. 'I think it's a very bad idea.'

'Walt! What on earth do you mean, *a bad idea?*'

'Exactly that.' He rose to his feet abruptly. 'I must go.'

'No,' she said, stepping in front of him, barring his way, 'you can't just leave it at that. You must tell me why.'

He moved around her and went out through the doorway. 'I don't have to explain it at all,' he said frostily.

★   ★   ★

For the following week she saw nothing of him and he made no attempt to contact her. However, after work on Friday evening when the telephone rang, Merri snatched it up, desperately hoping it would be Walt, but instead it was Prue speaking from the airport at Dubai.

'Merri, darling, I'm so glad to have caught you. We're at the airport awaiting a flight back to England. We should land sometime in the early hours but we intend spending the rest of the night in an hotel and coming home later in the morning. So, we shall probably be with you before noon. I can't give you the exact time, obviously. I'm so looking forward to seeing you, darling, I've missed you. It's so comforting to know you're there.'

'I've missed you, too. It will be wonderful to have you back.'

'Oh, Merri, I need to get back to Rafters. I shall feel then that I'm finally putting the past behind me and can start my life anew.'

There was obviously something seriously wrong, but before she had chance
to say anything to her aunt, the call
suddenly disconnected.

It left Merri feeling deeply disturbed.

★　★　★

But the next morning, thinking about
her aunt's words, she was so thankful
she'd gone ahead with purchasing the
new ponies and taking on the disabled
clients. If she hadn't, Prue might so
easily not have a home to return to.

She resolutely put all worrying
thoughts behind her and concentrated
upon the six disabled children already
mounted and eagerly awaiting setting
off from the stable yard. Once again, it
was a glorious morning, hot and still,
with a heat haze shimmering.

'Everybody ready?' she called, and
mounted Crispin. 'OK — ' she got no
further.

As one, the children's voices rang
out, gleefully, 'Let's ride.'

Smiling at their irrepressible high spirits, she led the ride down the lane to the forty-acre.

Tabby was standing by the gate. 'Couldn't keep away, you see,' she called.

'I wouldn't want you to,' Merri called back. 'But you'll get roped in to work if you're not careful.'

The children had all gone through into the field and Merri was preparing to ride after them when there was a screeching of brakes and a familiar battered Range Rover pulled up. Walt jumped out, his eyes narrowing as he saw the string of ponies. 'I couldn't believe you were serious. Do you know how damaging a fall could be for these children?' He glared at her. 'Well, do you?'

'Calm down, Walt. They aren't going to fall.'

'And just how can you be so sure? Simply riding is a risk.'

Tabby was listening to him with her head cocked to one side, eyes intent on his face. 'That's what the helpers are for,' she said placatingly. 'It's hardly the same as race riding.' Something in the tone of her last words made him swing round.

'Just what are you inferring?'

'I think you know perfectly well,' Tabby said sweetly. 'Perhaps it would be better though, if you told Merri. At least then she'd understand where you're coming from.'

A dull red flush stained his face. 'I don't need advice from you — ' His next words were lost.

Harry gave a shrill cry. 'Go down, go down.' He began to struggle to free his surgical boot from the stirrup iron and waved wildly to them.

Beatrice, in charge of Mr Chips, called out, 'Wait, wait, look out . . . Whoa, boy, steady.'

'What on earth . . . ' Merri dug her heels into Crispin's sides and cantered across the grass. Walt and Tabby, exchanging alarmed glances, raced after her. Harry cried out again, this time in fear, as losing his grip completely, he toppled from the pony's back and landed with a heavy thud on the grass.

Merri came alongside on Crispin, and grasped the pony's reins, making sure his hooves were well away from where the little boy lay.

Walt was the first to reach the child. He bent over him. 'Dear God, it's Harry!' His face lost its angry flush and turned chalk white.

'Don't pick him up, he may be injured,' Merri said, and slid out of the saddle, holding both sets of reins.

'You should never have risked him riding.' Walt was tight-lipped with anger.

'You don't have the right to dictate to me what I can and cannot do with Harry.'

'That's where you're wrong. I do. I'm his natural father.' Walt tenderly brushed a lock of hair from the child's forehead.

The shock of his words hit Merri like a punch in the solar plexus, totally winding her. 'You'd better explain,' she gasped.

'Later.'

Tabby had just reached them and now took over the two sets of reins.

Merri knelt down beside Harry and saw with great relief he was not unconscious as she'd thought but merely a little dazed and was already struggling to sit up. His wide eyes looked first at her and then at Walt. A big grin spread across his face and he scrambled awkwardly to his feet.

'Daddy, Daddy.' He flung his arms high and Walt scooped him up.

'Whoa, there, Harry boy. Are you all right?'

'It's just my knee,' he said.

'Your knee?' Walt's face mirrored his concern.

'Doesn't hurt much,' Harry put his hand down and rubbed his right kneecap. Walt's eyes met Merri's above the child's head. United with relief, they visibly relaxed.

'Have you come to see me ride,

Daddy? I'm on Mr Chips.'

'Yes, son. I know you are.'

Suddenly Harry started to wriggle. 'Go down, go down,' he shrilled and slid through Walt's arms back to the grass. 'Ride again.' He clutched at Mr Chips' bridle.

'Oh no,' said Walt. 'No you don't.'

Merri and Tabby exchanged glances. Tabby said gently, 'Let him, Walt, he needs to.'

'No chance. He's not getting back on.' He clutched hold of Harry's arm but the little boy began to tug and yell.

'Want to, want to, Daddy. Let me.'

'Even if it's only for a minute,' said Merri, 'you have to let him, Walt.'

Walt clenched his jaw, 'Don't you dare put him back on.'

'It's important he gets back on,' said Tabby, softly. 'You know it is.'

'One minute,' Walt compressed his lips and swung Harry up into the saddle. Instantly, the little boy's face was transformed and he dashed away the tears that had been trickling down his cheeks and smiled happily.

But no sooner had he settled himself and gathered up the reins than Megs shouted a warning, accompanied by a frantic flailing of her arm, 'Help! Wasps!'

'Don't! Flapping irritates them, they'll sting.' Walt's warning was too late.

Mr Chips standing patiently waiting, suddenly gave a shrill whinny and half-reared before putting in a massive buck.

'Hang on to him,' screamed Merri, and made a dive for the pony as he snatched himself free from Megs hold. But she couldn't catch him. He was away. Galloping down the side of the hedge along the forty-acre.

'If he goes through the boundary hedge,' gasped Tabby, 'he'll be straight onto the road.'

Merri ran a few steps, realised the futility of it and turned back for Crispin. But Walt, who had been standing rigid with fists clenched, suddenly vaulted into Crispin's saddle, dug his heels into the horse and set off in pursuit.

There was nothing any of them could do except hang onto the other ponies and try to keep them calm. They were all transfixed, watching Mr Chips galloping away with Harry clutching tightly both to the reins and the pony's flaxen mane. The other children, unaware of any danger, cheered and clapped. But Merri, who had never felt so helpless, watched in horror as the pony drew closer and closer to the boundary. If he ploughed through it, he'd be in traffic. She felt sick with fear.

But Crispin's speed far outmatched the little Shetland and he overhauled him rapidly. Racing alongside, Walt stretched out his arm and grabbed hold of Mr Chips' bridle. He quickly brought the pony's speed down to a canter, a trot and finally, to a stop.

Walt turned both animals and firmly holding Mr Chips' rein in one hand, walked Crispin back, whilst Harry, oblivious to the near disaster, sat astride

Mr Chips, beaming broadly and chattering away non-stop to his father. It was evident that the little boy had suffered no ill-effects.

Dizzy with relief, Merri, watched them drawing closer. Bracing herself however to withstand Walt's anger, she saw instead, an expression of totally relaxed contentment on his face, something, she realised with hindsight, he had never had before. It was not only his expression, but also his body language. That disturbing undercurrent of closed secretiveness she had always been uncomfortably aware of had totally disappeared. His face was open now, honest.

'Returned all in one piece,' Walt said as he dismounted.

'Well done indeed, lad,' said Tabby, and slapped his shoulder. 'Without your quick action, that could have been very nasty.'

'Amen to that,' Merri said. 'But I never realised just what a super rider Harry is. There're not many children who would have been able to stay on. And not only ride the pony out, but really enjoy doing it.' She turned to the little boy. 'Well done, Harry. That took a lot of nerve.' He beamed at her.

'Takes after his father,' said Tabby, and winked at Walt.

'Wasn't Mr Chips' fault,' Harry said earnestly. 'He bolted 'cos he got stung, Megs said.'

'He did?'

'Those dashed clegs,' said Tabby.

'Clegs?' His little face screwed up as Harry tried out this new word. 'What's clegs?'

'Horseflies.' Tabby ruffled his hair with her hand.

'No, Megs said it was a waps.'

His father smiled. 'Wasp, you mean.'

Harry nodded seriously. 'Yes, a waps, s'right.'

They were all trying not to smile. But his words had effectively dispelled any last lingering traces of tension.

Merri looked across and saw Walt watching her. He couldn't hide the depth of feeling in his eyes. It was primeval. Every cell in her body resonated to his unspoken message. Their eyes met and the magnetism between them was an almost tangible linking current.

It took an immense effort, but realising everybody was waiting for her instructions, she managed to withdraw her gaze.

'I think this is the moment,' she said, taking a very deep breath and gathering herself, 'when I'm going to be most unpopular and say it's time to return to the stables.'

Predictably, there was a chorus of protest from the children, including Harry. But holding up her hand and laughing, she continued, 'That's the bad news. The good news is, I'd love you all to come again next Saturday morning, and the ride will be absolutely free. What do you say?'

Once more, there was a chorus from them all but this time it was vigorously in favour.

'Everybody ready then?' She deliberately prompted them into yet another gleeful outburst. They didn't disappoint her.

'Let's ride!'

11

They were sitting drinking coffee in the kitchen at Rafters watching Harry rolling on the floor playing with Bentley and Timothy Whiskers.

The horses and ponies were safely stabled and the disabled children, after voting it the most exciting ride they'd ever been on, had finally been persuaded to go home.

'But I don't want to go home,' Harry had wailed. And both Megs and Beatrice agreed wholeheartedly that Harry should spend the rest of the day with his father.

Tabby, after much back-slapping, declared Walt a very brave man, and chuckling, told him to give her a few days notice so she could buy a new hat. Walt had turned a little pink around the ears and said he had no idea what she was talking about.

Now, surrounded by peace at last, Merri turned to Walt. 'I think you owe me an explanation. Or thinking about it, several explanations.' Walt took a sip of hot coffee.

'I know it's time to come clean,' he said and hesitated.

'You told me once to jump straight in when I wasn't sure how to tell you something. Perhaps you should take your own advice.'

'Didn't you ever wonder why you've never seen me actually ride a horse? Or how I came to have a limp?'

'Yes. I did wonder what had caused you to limp. It was obvious that you must have had an injury but I didn't want to embarrass you by asking.'

'It was at Cheltenham,' Walt said, staring down at his coffee. 'I had a crashing fall, broke my hip and . . . ' he raised his eyes and looked straight at her, 'lost my nerve.'

'Oh, Walt, I'm so sorry.' Merri covered his hand with her own. 'Couldn't you have told me? I sensed there was something you were holding back.'

'It's not something I'm prone to doing, disclosing personal and painful parts of myself.' He grinned wryly, 'You remember that little thing called trust? Well, this is to do with that other little thing, it's called the male ego. But we both agreed, no more misunderstandings so, I want to tell you everything.'

'Go on then, I'm listening.'

'I started my career as a jockey on the flat, rapidly got too weighty and after that, it was over the sticks, jump racing, but the money's pretty low.

'It was whilst I was flat racing that I met and married Sarah. Heaven knows why I did, she can't stand horses. However, as soon as our divorce came through — and she had custody of Harry — she married Mitchell. She'd been living with him since we'd split up. I don't blame her. I couldn't give her what she wanted, needed, a home and my constant attention.

We were living in rented accommodation that belonged to the trainer I worked for, couldn't afford our own place. And I'll admit it, the racing came first, had to in a way, well, I knew my flat racing days were about over, and I needed to earn money whilst I had the chance, so I used to go abroad winter racing.

'Sarah couldn't take it. She wanted me to give up racing. I couldn't, so I lost her. Ironic really, because afterwards I lost my nerve and had to give up.'

'If Sarah had waited though, things would have worked out for you both,' said Merri.

'Not really. You see, Sarah liked the good things in life and I couldn't supply them, not on what I earned.'

They were both silent for a moment then Walt said, 'In the end, I lost Sarah and my nerve.'

'But you haven't lost Harry.'

'I can't give him what he needs.'

'Why ever not? What is it he needs?'

'At this stage of his life, Harry needs his mother.'

Merri could not argue with this simple truth. 'Tabby was right, you are a brave man. Like my honey tree, sweet and very strong.'

'I'd always thought,' Walt went on, 'if and when I found the right woman, I'd buy a cottage and I'd marry her. Only then will I feel I've something to offer my son.'

'But you've so much to offer him now.'

'Seeing him come off today pressed my own button. I didn't think I'd ever get my nerve back.'

'Love is stronger than fear,' Merri murmured. 'And you love Harry very much.'

'He's not the only person I love.' The beautiful warmth in his eyes proved the truth of his words. He put down his coffee and reached for her hand. 'It's not the most romantic of settings but there's something I want to ask you — '

Before he could say more, there was

the sound of a vehicle driving in over the gravel drive. It pulled up outside the back door, there was the sound of voices and then a vehicle driving away.

Moments later, Prue followed by Matt appeared in the kitchen doorway.

'Prue!' Merri leaped to her feet in joy. 'Oh, Prue . . . '

'Darling, it's lovely to be home.'

'I've missed you . . . ' Merri stopped. Prue was carrying a new-born baby in her arms. She looked tired and drawn but managed to give both Merri and Walt a smile.

'This is going to come as a bit of a shock,' she said, 'but this little one,' and she bent her head and looked down lovingly at the tiny baby, 'this is Megan, my new granddaughter.'

And then they were all talking at once and Walt pulled out a kitchen chair and Prue sank down on it gratefully whilst he and Matt lugged in all the suitcases from the back porch.

'A small whisky, I think,' said Matt.

'You're starting a bit early in the day,' said Walt.

'Not for me, idiot,' grinned Matt. 'For Prue of course, but since you've put the idea in my head, why not? Let's all have one.' And thereupon went through to the sitting room and returned with the drinks tray.

Merri poured them each a generous measure. 'Whatever the rest of the story is, I think we should drink to your homecoming and wet the baby's head at the same time.' And the glasses were all raised.

Then Merri said, intuitively, 'Prue, would this little baby have anything to do with the little baby you were holding about thirty years ago called Ella?'

Prue looked up in astonishment. 'However did you come to find out?'

'I didn't really. It was the kitten, Timothy Whiskers. He knocked your jewellery box flying and there was a photograph in the base of it that slipped out.'

'Of course you're right, my darling,'

said Prue. 'I had a baby when I was seventeen, couldn't keep her of course, a long, long time ago now, things were different.' Prue took a sip of whisky. 'A couple adopted her and they subsequently went out to live in Dubai. Ella actually traced me, because she was in desperate need. Perhaps, if she hadn't been, she wouldn't have wanted to know me.'

'Don't be an idiot,' said Merri.

Prue smiled gratefully. 'Well, who knows?'

'Where is Ella now?'

Matt put a hand on Prue's shoulder and squeezed his fingers. The gesture was not lost upon Merri and Walt.

'Don't answer me, if you don't want to, Prue. It's quite OK.'

'No, life's made up of sadness and of happiness,' said Prue. 'Both the same thing really, without one you cannot have the other. You have to accept it. I have to accept that Ella has gone, she's died . . . cancer . . . ' she bit her lip, unshed tears brimming in her eyes.

'But,' she said briskly now, 'she didn't leave me bereft. Just before she died, Megan was born by caesarean section. I thank God that Ella survived two more days. Enough to know that Megan was perfectly healthy, enough to hold her, love her — and then pass her on to me.'

There was silence.

'What about the baby's father?' asked Merri, finally.

'A married man, and of course, he didn't want to know,' Prue sighed. 'Ella made the same mistake that I did.'

There was silence again — the mood sombre.

Then a little voice said, 'Daddy, I want to go . . . ' and Harry crawled out from beneath the kitchen table and looked earnestly at Walt. 'Toilet, Daddy?'

When, tension released and atmosphere lightened, Walt returned from the bathroom leading Harry by the hand, Prue said, 'Well now, aren't you going to introduce me — Daddy?'

'Sorry, Prue,' grinned Walt. 'Meet my son, Harry.'

'My word, you kept that quiet.' Her eyebrows lifted. Then she looked down at the little boy, her voice softening, 'Hello Harry, darling. I'm so pleased to meet you.'

Harry looked down at the floor, shyly. Walt hunkered beside him and put an arm around the little boy's shoulders. 'Say hello to Prue,' he prompted.

Lifting those enormous eyes, he whispered, ' 'Lo, Prue.' And dived back under the table with Bentley.

Matt lifted the whisky decanter. 'If I may,' he said, 'I'd like to propose another toast. It seems to be a day of surprises. But I'd like you two to raise a glass with Prue and I and wish us well, because Prue has done me the honour of agreeing to become my wife.'

Merri flung her arms around Prue. 'How wonderful for you. Oh Prue, I'm so, so pleased.'

'You have my full commiseration, Uncle,' said Walt, with a straight face.

'Are you all coming to live here?' asked Merri.

'No,' said Matt, 'no, Prue and I are going to live at Chessington's and we're bringing Megan up as our own child.'

'But Cornfields Stables are just beginning to take off,' said Merri, 'And what about Rafters?'

'I won't be needing Rafters any more,' said Prue. 'What about you staying on permanently, Merri?'

'You really mean it, Prue?' Merri's eyes were shining, 'I love Rafters. But, it's a big place on my own.'

Prue looked across at Walt who smiled back. 'I don't see that being an obstacle, do you?'

'To be honest, Prue,' Walt said, 'you just pipped me to the winning post, coming in through the backdoor at that moment. Five minutes later and who knows, it could have been a double celebration.'

Everybody turned to look at Merri, who blushed furiously.

'I don't recall being asked,' she said, deliberately evasively.

Walt held out his hand to her. 'Would

you mind accompanying me down to the stables? I don't think the ponies will understand what I'm talking about. And there's a question I want to ask you.'

Merri, still blushing, took his hand. 'Why not? And I'm glad the ponies won't understand because I might just have an answer to give you.'

We do hope that you have enjoyed reading this large print book.

Did you know that all of our titles are available for purchase?

We publish a wide range of high quality large print books including:
Romances, Mysteries, Classics General Fiction Non Fiction and Westerns

Special interest titles available in large print are:
The Little Oxford Dictionary Music Book, Song Book · Hymn Book, Service Book

Also available from us courtesy of Oxford University Press:
Young Readers' Dictionary (large print edition) Young Readers' Thesaurus (large print edition)

For further information or a free brochure, please contact us at:
Ulverscroft Large Print Books Ltd., The Green, Bradgate Road, Anstey, Leicester, LE7 7FU, England. Tel: (00 44) **0116 236 4325 Fax:** (00 44) **0116 234 0205**